Lost In Time

By
KingELOTheGod

(Ecclesiastes 3:1)
To everything there is a season, and a time
for every purpose under heaven

(Book Description)

Michael thought he was an ordinary man living an unremarkable life—until a mysterious force catapulted him across the fabric of time. From ancient civilizations to futuristic worlds, Michael witnesses pivotal moments in history, experiencing humanity's triumphs and tragedies firsthand. Along the way, he encounters Aelira, a time traveler with secrets of her own, whose role in his journey becomes increasingly enigmatic. Through battles in the distant past, harrowing events of war, and glimpses of a utopian future, Michael discovers that his choices ripple across time in ways he never imagined. As he grapples with the gravity of his actions and the truth about Aelira's identity, Michael must confront the ultimate question: Can one life truly change the course of history? Threads of Time: A Journey Through Eternity is a gripping exploration of destiny, humanity, and the enduring impact of the choices we make. Perfect for fans of time-travel adventures, historical epics, and stories that ponder the intricacies of fate, this novel will leave readers questioning their own place in the grand tapestry of existence. One man. Endless eras.
The power of choice will determine humanity's future.

(The Awakening)

In my present time New York City never truly slept, and neither did I and not because I was restless or insomniac or anything like that, but because my nights were filled with something extraordinary and in my current year 2025, most seventeen-year-olds in New York are glued to their phones or sneaking out to parties, while I'm traversing the world in ways they can't even imagine. And my bedroom is a small sanctuary in a city that thrives on chaos and plus, the walls are plastered with posters of bands that I no longer listen to, as a fading reminder of my fleeting teenage interests. And my desk is always cluttered with textbooks, notebooks, and half-finished art projects—and evidence that I'm a good student when I can focus. But none of that matters when the lights go out.

Then I remembered the time of the night that changed everything and it was 11:47p.m and the glow of the city seeped through the cracks of my curtains, and the muffled hum of traffic served as my background score. Then as I sat cross-legged on my bed, with my hands resting lightly on my knees, I closed my eyes breathing in, as I counted to four and then I breathed out, while counting to eight. And I've done this so many times now that my mind detaches almost instantly, slipping away from the confines of my body like a hand pulling free from a glove. And the first sensation is weightlessness. And my body feels distant, like a forgotten shell, as my astral form rises. Then I glance back and I see myself— Michael Carter, the skinny kid with messy brown hair and a perpetually furrowed brow—sitting motionless on the bed. Then a faint glow surrounds my physical self, and a tether that connects me to my earthly anchor, But I don't linger. I push off, gliding effortlessly through the ceiling of my family's apartment. And in moments, I'm soaring above the city, with the lights stretching out beneath me like a luminous map. And the Empire State Building stands proud and defiant in the distance, while the Hudson River reflects the glittering skyline like a shimmering ribbon.

"Where to tonight?" I murmur to myself, with the sound of my voice echoing in the empty vastness around me. And my first stop was the Serengeti. Then with a single thought, I propelled myself forward, then the urban sprawl of New York dissolved into a swirling blur. Then when the world sharpens again, I hovered above a vast golden plain, with the air shimmering with heat. And a herd of wild beasts grazed below, with their movements fluid and rhythmic. Then I drift closer, and careful not to disrupt the scene even though I know they can't see me, I still felt an odd reverence for this moment.

Then the distant roar of a lion catches my attention, and I pivot to see the predator stalking its prey and I could watch this for hours, but tonight I'm restless and there's more to see. So I think of the Northern Lights, and in an instant, I'm there. Then the icy expanse of the Arctic stretches out below me, with the air crisp and biting even in this astro form. And the auroras dance above, ribbons of green, purple, and blue weaving through the night sky, and it's breathtaking, and even for someone who's seen it a dozen of times. sometimes, I think about staying in one of these places, but I always return to the tether—the invisible thread that keeps me tied to my body. Because without it, I would be lost.

So my next stop is Tokyo, and the city is alive, and its streets buzzing with activity even at this late hour. So I hover above Shibuya Crossing, watching the sea of people move in perfect chaos. And neon signs flash advertisements in bold colors, with the kanji characters unfamiliar yet fascinating to me. And a young couple pauses in the middle of the crosswalk to snap a selfie, and I can't help but smile. So I thought to myself that this is my secret and my gift, and while others dream, I explore. Then eventually, the pull of my body grew stronger. And it always does after about an hour, like a gentle tug reminding me of my limits. And with a sigh, I let the scenes around me dissolve, and the sounds and colors fading into the void. Then when I opened my eyes, I was back in my bedroom. And the clock read 12:48 a.m., and the city's hum is as steady as ever. So I stretch my arms, feeling the weight of my physical form settle back over me.

Then as I laid back down, staring at the ceiling, I couldn't help but wonder if I can do this now, at seventeen, what else is out there for me to discover. Then at about 2:00 a.m. New York City was a little quieter, but my night was far from over, and I thought I'd call it a quits for the night, but something inside me itches for more. Then my body feels sluggish, and weighed down by the pull of sleep, but my astral form was restless. So, I close my eyes, and I let my breathing slow, then I slip free once again. But this time, I don't hesitate. And the moment I leave my body, I shoot upward, high above the city until with the familiar skyline becoming a grid of light, and the earth itself curved in my view. And from this height the planet looks alive, like veins of civilization glowing against the darker swaths of forest and ocean. And it's breathtaking, even now, after years of doing this.

"Let me go see the pyramids," I Then whisper to myself, and with a thought, I'm there. And the cool desert air greeted me as I float above the sands of Giza. And the Great Pyramid looms large in the moonlight, with its limestone surface weathered yet majestic. And the Sphinx stands guard nearby, with its enigmatic expression frozen in time. And below, a group of tourists sat in a circle with flashlights sharing ghost stories under the stars. Then I drift closer to listen, but their words are drowned out by the desert wind. And something about ancient places like this always humbles me. Because these structures have stood for thousands of years, bearing witness to empires rising and falling. And here I was, an uninvited observer, passing through their shadows like a ghost.

Then from Egypt, I decide to head somewhere colder then with a single thought I'm brought back to Antarctica again, where the stark whiteness of the ice is almost blinding. And the air here feels different this time. But I hover above a colony of emperor penguins, and their black and white bodies huddled together for warmth. And a chick waddles out from the group, with its fluffy gray feathers ruffled by the wind and I noticed that I was seeing a different part of Antarctica then the penguin trips and falls, and I chuckle softly to myself. Then further out, I see a research station, with its lights glowing faintly against the endless snow. And inside, a group of scientists are gathered around a table, laughing and sharing and what looked like instant ramen. And their laughter felt so warm in this frozen landscape, and for a moment, I wonder what it would be like to join them, to live a life so remote and simple.

But then the pull of exploration calls me elsewhere and I still remained in full control. So next, I visited Rio de Janeiro. And the city was alive even at this late hour with samba music drifting through the air and the glow of streetlights illuminating the narrow, winding roads. Then I float above the iconic Christ the Redeemer statue, with its massive arms outstretched over the city as if in eternal embrace. And below the favelas are quiet, with their vibrant colors muted in the darkness. Then I see a soccer game happening on a small field near the beach, with players shouting in Portuguese as they chase the ball under makeshift floodlights. So I hover for a while, enjoying the energy of the match and it amazes me how life continues, no matter the hour or the place.

Then from Rio, I think of something even more exotic. "The Great Barrier Reef," I say aloud, then in an instant I'm underwater. And the colors here are unreal—with brilliant corals in shades of pink, orange, and purple stretching out in every direction and teeming with life and with schools of fish darting around me, with their scales shimmering like liquid rainbows. Then a sea turtle glides past, unbothered by my presence, and I follow it for a while, marveling at the effortless grace of its movements. Then I think to myself that this world beneath the waves feels like an entirely different planet. And the hum of the ocean fills my senses, and for a moment, I forget that I'm not actually here, and that my body is still lying in a darkened in a bedroom thousands of miles away.

And time feels strange during these journeys. Minutes can feel like hours, and yet when I return, barely any time has passed. But still, I know I've been traveling for a while now, and the tether to my body grows heavier with each passing moment. So before I head back, I make one final stop to the Himalayas. And the air here was sharp and thin, with the peaks piercing the heavens like jagged teeth. Then I float above the snowy ridges, the silence almost deafening. In the distance, as I see a line of climbers ascending on Mount Everest, with their tiny figures dwarfed by the sheer magnitude of the mountain. Then I approach the summit, where prayer flags flutter in the icy wind. And the view from up here is staggering—and the world stretched out below me, endless and vast but it feels like the top of everything, and a place where time itself might stop, But my body calls me home. And the tether tugs gently but insistently, and I let myself be drawn back. Then the world around me dissolved into darkness, and when I open my eyes, I was back in my room. And the clock read 2:12 a.m. and my limbs felt heavy as I stretch, but my mind is alive with everything I've seen like the pyramids, the ice, and the coral reefs—and they're all imprinted in my memory, vivid and surreal. Then as I laid back down, I stared at the ceiling, and I wondered where I'll go next. Because the world felt so much larger when you can see it all, but for now it felt good to be home.

(Astral Accident)

Then it happened and I always thought I had control with my years of practice, and countless nights spent perfecting the art of astral projection—and I thought I mastered it at least that's what I told myself. And I thought the tethers invisible thread connecting me to my body, was unbreakable, but tonight, something feels… wrong. And it started small with a faint resistance as I try to leave my body, like a rubber band stretched too tight, and I usually, slip out effortless, like sliding through water. But tonight, I feel an odd tension. But I dismiss it at first, chalking it up to being overtired. Because I've been pushing myself hard lately, by traveling further, and staying out longer so maybe my mind is just fatigued I thought.

But as I rise from my bed, the tension follows me. And I notice that it's subtle, like a whisper at the back of my mind, telling me something isn't right. But I still ignore it because I'm Michael Carter, the kid who can see the world without leaving his room and nothing can stop me I thought. Then I continued floating above my apartment, and I look down at the familiar glow of New York City. And the streets were quieter now, and the usual chaos muted by the late hour was gone. But the sight, usually comforting, feels off tonight. The lights seem dimmer, the air heavier. Shaking off the unease, But I push forward anyway.

"Let's me start with Paris," I say aloud, trying to inject some enthusiasm into my voice. So I blink, and I'm there. And the Eiffel Tower rises before me, with its lights sparkling against the dark Parisian sky, and couples stroll along the Seine, with their laughter soft and melodic, and it's beautiful, as always, but the tension in my chest hasn't eased and if anything, it's worse now. So I try to move closer to the tower, but something holds me back it's as if the tether to my body is tightening, pulling me in the opposite direction, then panic flickers in my mind because this has never happened before and usually, I can move freely, and untethered except for the faint connection that keeps me grounded. But now, I feel like I'm on a leash that's being yanked, hard.

"What the hell is going on?" I mutter, trying to push forward. And then, it happens. A sudden, violent tug jerks me away from Paris. Then the world blurs around me, colors and shapes melting into an unrecognizable swirl. And I feel like I'm being dragged through a tunnel, faster than I've ever traveled before. Then my chest tightens, and for the first time, I feel something I've never associated with astral projection and that is pain. Then when the world sharpens again, I'm not where I intended to be. But instead I'm in the middle of a dense jungle, with the air thick with humidity, and the sounds of birds and insects are deafening, and the canopy above blocks out most of the moonlight. Panic bubbles up as I try to orient myself. "This isn't right," I whisper, with my voice trembling, because I've

5

never arrived somewhere unintentionally before. And my journeys have always been deliberate, guided by my thoughts. But this place feels foreign, hostile. So I try to leave, to think of home and pull myself back to New York, but nothing happens, and the tether, my lifeline, feels weak now, like a thread unraveling.

"Focus, Michael," I tell myself, closing my eyes and trying again. But this time, I'm yanked violently into another location. Then the jungle vanishes, and its replaced by a vast, barren desert with the sun beating down mercilessly, and the heat searing even in my astral form. And the sand stretches endlessly in every direction, and I feel utterly alone. So I scream into the void, frustration and fear mingling. "What is happening to me?" Then the tether tugs again, and I'm pulled into yet another place, and this time, I'm underwater with a coral reef surrounding me, vibrant and teeming with life. But the beauty is overshadowed by the suffocating weight of my situation. So I try to swim upward, to escape, but the water feels thick and unyielding, as if it's trying to trap me. And each time I try to regain control, I'm dragged somewhere else. And a snowy mountaintop was next, then a crowded marketplace. And a dark forest, and the transitions were disorienting, and the tug of the tether grew weaker with every jump.

And then, for a terrifying moment, I feel nothing. No tether. No connection to my body. Just endless space and the crushing realization that I might be lost. "Pull it together," I whisper, with my voice barely hearable over the pounding of my thoughts. "You've done this a hundred times. You know how to get back." But do I? So again I close my eyes, reaching deep inside myself for any semblance of connection. And then I feel it—a faint pulse, like a heartbeat, guiding me. It's faint, but it's there. Then with every ounce of focus, I follow it, ignoring the swirling chaos around me. Then the world shifts one last time, and I find myself hovering above my bedroom with a relief that washes over me as I see my body below still and waiting. But as I try to re-enter, the resistance is back, stronger than ever. And it's like trying to push through a wall that doesn't want to let me in. So, I press harder, gritting my teeth. Slowly, agonizingly, then I feel myself sinking back into my body and the sensations return—the weight of my limbs, and the steady rhythm of my heartbeat. Then when I finally open my eyes, I'm drenched in sweat, my chest heaving. And It's 3:12 a.m. with my room feeling stifling, as the air too thick to breathe. I sit up, gripping the edges of my bed as my mind races. What just happened? Why did my control slip? And most importantly, what if it happens again? Because for the first time since I started astral projecting now I felt afraid.

Then by 5:12 a.m., the city was quiet. And the soft hum of New York's pre-dawn stillness seeped through the cracks in my window. And really I should be asleep, but I can't shake the feeling of what just happened earlier. And my breathing is uneven now, and my hands trembling as I sit cross-legged on my bed.

6

What went wrong? I've been asking myself that question for hours, replaying every moment of my projection. Because the sudden resistance, the erratic jumps—none of it makes sense. And this has never happened before. Not even once. But curiosity is a dangerous thing. And as scared as I am, I can't stop thinking about the tether, the faint pulse I felt in the void that was weakening? Or worse, was it severed altogether, and I didn't realize?

Then I thought "I need to try again," I whisper into the darkness. And the rational part of my brain screams at me to stop, to wait until I've had more time to recover, but I don't listen because the pull to know, and to understand, is stronger than my fear. So I close my eyes and breathe in deeply. In for four, out for eight. This ritual is second nature by now. Then my body grows lighter, as my senses sharpen. Then the weight of the physical world fades away, and soon, I'm hovering above myself again. And everything seems normal at first. As my body is still, and my tether intact, and the faint glow around my physical form reassures me but maybe it was a fluke, I tell myself. A one-time glitch I thought. So I push off, gliding through the ceiling and into the open air above the city. And the skyline was breathtaking in the pre-dawn light, a soft glow rising on the horizon. And for a moment, I let myself believe that everything is fine, and that I'm in control again.

But the feeling doesn't last and the first sign of trouble is subtle: a faint tug at the edge of my consciousness, like an invisible hand pulling me sideways and It's not the familiar tether; this is something else, something... wrong again. "No," I mutter, trying to shake it off then I focus on the city below, willing myself to stay anchored. But the pull grows stronger. And then it happens again, and without warning this time, because I was yanked violently from my position, and the city dissolved into a blur. So I try to resist, to fight the force dragging me, but it's too strong. Then my surroundings shift, and suddenly I'm somewhere else entirely.

Now I was in a battlefield with the air thick with smoke and the deafening roar of gunfire. Soldiers run past me, shouting orders in a language I don't recognize. Then the ground trembles as an explosion erupts nearby, the heat scorching even in my astral form. "What the hell?" I gasp, spinning around in confusion. I don't belong here. This isn't a place I would ever choose to visit. But before I can make sense of it, the tug returns, yanking me away again. But this time, I'm in a bustling marketplace. And the smells of spices and cooked meat fill the air, mingling with the chatter of merchants and customers as the sun beated down harshly, and I recognize the architecture—it's ancient, Middle Eastern, maybe but I barely have time to register the scene before I'm pulled again.

And now, I'm underwater, surrounded by the crushing silence of the deep ocean, and the water is dark, with the pressure immense even in this form. Then shapes move in the distance, massive and slow but I don't want to know what they

7

are. "Stop it!" I shout, though there's no one to hear me. Then I noticed that the transitions come faster now. A dense jungle. A futuristic city with glowing skyscrapers. Then a barren wasteland under a blood-red sky. And each place is more jarring than the last, and the tether—my lifeline—feels weaker with every jump.

Then I try to focus again, and ground myself, but my thoughts are scattered as panic creeps in, and I feel like I'm unraveling, my sense of self slipping away. Then the next shift lands me in a vast, featureless void where there's no sound, no light, just an endless expanse of nothingness. And for a terrifying moment, I wonder if this is it—if I've been cut loose entirely, and lost forever. But then, faintly, I feel it: the tether. It's barely there, like a single thread in a raging storm, but it's enough. So I grab hold of it with everything I have, pulling myself toward the faint pulse of my body but the void resists, and its emptiness clinging to me, but I push through.

Then when I finally open my eyes, I'm back in my room and my body feels heavy, almost suffocating, and my head throbs with a dull, persistent ache. And the clock read 5:27 a.m. and only fifteen minutes had passed, but it felt like hours to me. So I laid back on the bed, staring at the ceiling as my heart races and something is happening to me, something I don't understand an my control is slipping, and the thought terrifies me because for the first time in years, I consider the possibility that this gift, this power I've taken for granted, might also be a curse.

(Ancient Egypt)

As more time passed the clock now read 6:30 a.m., and I was still wide awake, staring at the ceiling like it held answers and my body was exhausted, but my mind buzzed with unease. Because the earlier projections had been chaotic—unlike anything I'd experienced before. But still, I couldn't let it go. And I thought that this time would be different. And I told myself that over and over, like a mantra. So I'd take it slow, focus harder, and regain control. Because after all, I'd spent years mastering astral projection. So whatever went wrong tonight was a fluke so I thought because it had to be.

Then I sat cross-legged on my bed again, inhaling deeply and exhaling slowly with my heartbeat steadied, as my surroundings softened, and once again, I felt the familiar pull of separation. Then my spirit began to rise, and the connection to my physical form intact and solid. And for the first time in hours, I felt a flicker of hope. But then, it happened again. And the tug came again, that horrible, relentless force. But this time it was different, it wasn't dragging me through dimensions it was dragging me out entirely this time. And before I could fight it, I felt a sickening lurch, like my entire being was yanked through a needle's eye.

Then there was no blur, no gradual transition. Because one second, I was in my room; and the next, I was somewhere completely different. So I stood in the middle of a vast desert as the sun blazed down from a cloudless sky, as the heat wrapping around me like a suffocating blanket. And sand stretched endlessly in every direction, and in the distance, I saw massive stone structures loomed—pyramids. Then I noticed that this wasn't an astral projection but this time it felt real. Because I could feel the sand under my feet, sand smell the dry, baked earth, and also hear the faint rustle of the desert wind. And oddly my body was here, not just my spirit unlike the last times.

"What the hell?" I whispered, with my voice trembling. As my throat felt parched, and my skin already prickling from the sun. Then I turned in a slow circle, trying to make sense of it. And I noticed that the pyramids were unmistakable, but they weren't the weathered ruins I'd seen in pictures because the pyramids that I was currently seeing were pristine, and their limestone surfaces were gleaming white under the sunlight. And workers moved around them hauling massive blocks of stone with ropes and sledges.

Then my heart pounded as the realization hit me because this wasn't modern day Egypt this was ancient Egypt. And before I could fully process it, a shout rang out behind me. So I turned to see a group of men approaching, with their dark skin glistening with sweat. And they wore simple linen garments and carried tools that looked like they belonged in a museum. Then one of them froze

9

when he saw me, and his eyes widen with disbelief. As he dropped to his knees, bowing low to the ground and the others followed suit, murmuring words I didn't understand.

"What... what are you doing?" I stammered, taking a step back. Then one of them looked up at me, and his expression was a mix of awe and fear. "Amun-Ra," he whispered, the word thick with reverence. Then I froze. They thought I was a god but even more odd was that they could see me. And before I could argue or correct them, they began to chant, with their voices rising in unison. Then within minutes, more people arrived—workers, villagers, and even priests. And they all surrounded me, with their faces lit with wonder. Then I tried to speak, to explain, but my words were drowned out by their chants. Then I was swept away, and led to a temple carved into the side of a cliff and the air inside was cooler, heavy with the scent of incense. Then priests draped me in fine linen and adorned me with gold jewelry, with their hands trembling as they worked and then I knew that I was really in ancient Egypt.

Then for the next few days—or was it weeks?—I lived as a god among them. And they brought me food, exotic fruits and roasted meats. And they showed me their rituals, their prayers, their offerings. And I witnessed ceremonies that modern archaeologists could only dream of seeing. But the awe and reverence quickly became suffocating. As I couldn't go anywhere without an entourage. And people bowed as I passed afraid to meet my eyes. And every word that I spoke was treated like divine wisdom, even when I was just asking for water. So I tried to adapt to their world, to learn their language and customs, but it was exhausting and the weight of their expectations was crushing because I wasn't a god. I was just a scared kid who'd been thrown into a world that he didn't belong in.

And then there was the constant fear—fear that I'd never get back home. And every night, I tried to project again, to slip out of this body and return to my own time. But nothing worked. The tether, my connection to my real life, felt severed. I was trapped here, in a body that didn't feel like mine, in a time that wasn't mine. Then one night, as I sat on the temple steps under a sky full of stars, I felt the crushing weight of my situation because the chants and rituals had stopped for the evening, and for the first time in weeks, I was alone.

"What am I supposed to do?" I whispered to the stars. But there was no answer, of course Just the distant sounds of the desert—crickets, the soft whisper of the wind. But then, I felt it. A faint tug, like the pulse of a heartbeat and my tether wasn't gone after all I thought. Then hope surged through me as I closed my eyes, focusing on that faint connection and it was weak, like a dying ember, but it was there. Slowly, carefully, so I began to pull.

Then the world around me faded, and the sounds of ancient Egypt dissolved into silence. And the heat of the desert was replaced by the cool stillness of my bedroom. Then when I opened my eyes, I was back so I thought. So I laid there for a long time, staring at the ceiling, as my chest heaving with relief that I was home, but I couldn't shake the feeling of the sand under my feet, the weight of the gold around my neck, and the sound of their chants plus I had been gone for weeks, but here, barely an hour had passed. "What's happening to me?" I whispered. But I didn't have an answer. And all I knew was that something had changed. I wasn't just projecting anymore. I was traveling, physically with my physical body now, and I had no idea how to stop it.

Then when I woke up I expected to see the familiar ceiling of my bedroom, or the glow of the early morning light filtering through the blinds. But instead, I was greeted by the blinding glare of the sun and the golden sandstone walls of the temple. Then my heart sank because I realized that I was back in ancient Egypt. "No," I whispered, sitting up abruptly. The fine linen robes they'd draped me in rustled with the movement, and the heavy gold collar around my neck felt suffocating. Then I scrambled to my feet, and the cold stone beneath me grounding me in a way I didn't expect. Then I realized that this wasn't a dream after all and that I never really made it home but I actually was just dreaming that I made it home. And that the previous days—or weeks?—had been a blur but they were real. So I'd tried so hard to focus on the tether, and the faint connection that had pulled me back to my own time before. But now, there was nothing and the thread that had anchored me was gone completly.

And then a low hum reached my ears, and a sound that started softly but grew louder and more distinct. Chanting. As the priests were coming. So, I stepped out onto the balcony of the temple, with my heart pounding as I looked out over the sprawling city. And the sun was just beginning to rise, as it was bathing in the sand and stone in hues of gold and crimson was below me, and a sea of people had gathered, their faces turned upward in expectation.

"Amun-Ra!" they cried, their voices merging into a thunderous chorus. Then I gripped the stone railing, with my knuckles white. Because they still thought that I was a god. Or some kind of deity, come to walk among them. And no matter how many times I tried to correct them, to explain that I wasn't divine, they wouldn't hear it. But to them, my strange appearance and my sudden arrival from nowhere were all the proof that they needed. Then the priests arrived, bowing low before me as they offered trays of food and drink. Then one of them—a man with sharp eyes and a solemn expression—spoke in a language I still barely understood, but I caught enough to piece it together.

"Great Amun-Ra, the people await your blessing." Then I wanted to scream and I wanted to grab him and shake him and shout that I wasn't who they thought I was. But I knew it wouldn't work and they wouldn't believe me. And what if I pushed too hard? What if they turned on me? So, I did what I'd been doing for weeks. I played the part. And I stepped forward, raising my hands as the crowd below erupted in cheers. And the sheer noise of it made my skin crawl, but I forced myself to keep going because I didn't have a choice. Then for what felt like hours, I was paraded through the city. And they showed me their markets, their workshops, their homes. And everywhere I went, people knelt, pressing their foreheads to the ground in reverence. And even children brought me flowers; as merchants offered me goods.

It should have felt incredible—being worshiped, treated like royalty. But all I felt was trapped. As days turned into weeks the routine was the same: wake up in the temple, endure endless rituals, be paraded through the city. And at night, I would sit on the temple steps, staring up at the stars and wondering if I'd ever see my home for real again.

Then the priests tried to teach me their language, and I learned quickly—probably out of necessity more than anything else because understanding them made it easier to navigate their world, but it also made their devotion even more overwhelming. Then one evening, as I sat alone in the temple courtyard, a young priest approached me. His name was Setek, and unlike the others, he didn't seem afraid of me. "Great Amun-Ra," he said softly, kneeling before me. "Naw just Michael," I replied, as the words slipping out before I could stop myself. Then he looked up, confusion flickering across his face. "Michael?" then I nodded, as the sound of my own name grounding me for the first time in what felt like ages. "That's my name. I'm not... I'm not Amun-Ra." Then Setek tilted his head, studying me with an intensity that made me uncomfortable. "But you came from the sky. You appeared in the temple of the sun. Who else could you be?" Then I opened my mouth to argue, but the words caught in my throat. Because how could I explain what had happened? That I wasn't a god, but a kid from the 21st century who had somehow ended up here through no fault of his own? So Instead, I said nothing and Setek didn't press. He simply nodded and left me alone, with his expression thoughtful. And that night, I laid awake, staring at the stars as my mind churned with questions like why was this happening and why couldn't I go back? Or worse was I being punished for something? Or was this all some sort of a test?

Then the days grew heavier, and the weight of their worship crushing me. But I tried to adapt, to blend into their world, but it was impossible. And their reverence was constant, with their expectations suffocating. And I felt like I was losing myself, becoming less Michael and more of the god they wanted me to be. Then one night, I couldn't take it anymore. And I climbed to the top of the temple, as the city spread out before me in the moonlight. The pyramids loomed in the distance, and their sharp angles cutting into the night sky. Then I closed my eyes and focused, searching desperately for the tether. Because I knew it had to be there, somewhere, faint but alive. I pushed everything else out of my mind—the heat, the noise, the weight of their worship—and reached deep into the void. Then for a moment, I felt it. A flicker, like a distant heartbeat and it was my tether. But then, it was gone and I sank to my knees, the realization hitting me like a blow to the chest because I was stuck here. Then weeks turned into what felt like months. And the line between who I was and who they thought I was blurred as I played the part, and gave the blessings, and also performed the rituals. But inside, I was breaking because I didn't know if I would ever get back home.

(The Year 3025)

Then suddenly it happened again, and I was lying in the courtyard of the temple in Ancient Egypt, staring up at the endless expanse of stars and exhaustion weighed me down, both physical and emotional. And I couldn't tell how long I'd been there—days or weeks? Because time seemed to blur, stretching into something unrecognizable. And I was too tired to fight the pull when it came and the now-familiar sensation of being yanked out of place swept over me. As my surroundings distorted, and the stars above spinning into streaks of light. Then the air around me grew colder, sharper, until suddenly... I wasn't in Egypt anymore.

Then when I opened my eyes, I was surrounded by gleaming skyscrapers that towered impossibly high, and their surfaces shimmering with colors I'd never seen before, and roads that floated mid-air, intersecting at impossible angles, with vehicles speeding by silently, their designs sleek and otherworldly. As the air buzzed with an electric hum, and the faint sound of machinery humming in the distance. Then it hit me almost immediately because I was sure that this wasn't the past and that must be the future but what year though I thought to myself.

Then I sat up slowly, with my hands brushing against the ground—no, not ground. It was smooth, metallic, like polished steel. And beneath the surface, faint lights pulsed rhythmically, forming intricate patterns that shifted as I moved. "What the..." I muttered, standing on unsteady legs. And my voice sounded strange in the crisp, artificial air. And around me, people—or what I assumed were people—moved with purpose. And they wore fitted garments that seemed to glow faintly, with colors shifting as they walked. And some of them floated above the ground, with their feet never touching the surface. And their eyes glowed faintly too, an eerie but mesmerizing effect.

"Excuse me?" I called out to one of them, but they didn't stop they didn't even look at me it was as if I didn't exist. So I tried again, stepping in front of someone—a tall figure with silver hair and skin so smooth it looked like porcelain. "Hey! Where am I?" Then They paused, with their glowing eyes scanning me briefly. Then, without a word, they continued walking, and passing through me like I was nothing more than air. And a chill ran down my spine. Then I thought to myself was I a ghost here? Or had I projected again instead of fully teleporting? But no—because my body felt real still. And I could feel the cool metallic surface beneath my feet, and the faint vibrations in the air.

So as I wandered through the city, the enormity of the future unfolded around me. And massive holograms flickered in the sky, displaying symbols and images I couldn't comprehend. And buildings seemed to breathe, their surfaces shifting and rearranging as if alive. And the sky above wasn't blue—it was a deep, endless black, dotted with stars that seemed unnervingly close. "What is this place?" I whispered to myself. Then my exploration led me to what appeared to be a marketplace—or its futuristic equivalent. Because stalls floated mid-air, displaying wares that defied explanation: and glowing orbs that pulsed with energy, with devices that rearranged themselves when touched, and containers holding swirling liquids that seemed to defy gravity.

Then as I approached one of the stalls, the merchant—a being with four arms and skin that shimmered like liquid mercury—spoke in a language I couldn't understand. And their voice was melodic, almost hypnotic. "I don't understand," I said, shaking my head. Then the merchant tilted their head, studying me. Then, with a wave of one of their arms, a small device floated toward me. And it attached itself to my temple with a soft click, and suddenly, their words became clear. "You're not from here, are you?" they asked, their tone curious. "No," I admitted. "I don't even know where 'here' is." Then the merchant nodded, their expression unreadable. "You're in Solara City, on Earth. But you're... out of sync." "Out of sync?" I echoed, confusion knotting my stomach. "Yes. You're not aligned with this timeline." They leaned closer, their eyes narrowing. "You don't belong here." I wanted to argue, but the truth of their words settled heavy in my chest. And I didn't belong here just like I didn't belong in Ancient Egypt also.

Then the merchant handed me a small, glowing orb. "Take this. It will protect you... for now." "Protect me from what?" I asked, but they didn't answer they simply turned back to their wares, their interest in me already fading. Then I clutched the orb tightly as I continued through the city. The more I explored, the more alien everything felt and time seemed to move differently here, the days and nights blending together in a disorienting cycle.

Then weeks started to pass—or at least it felt like weeks. So I tried to adapt, to understand this world, but it was overwhelming. Because the technology was lightyears beyond anything I could comprehend, and the people—if they were even still people—were so far removed from humanity as I knew it. And I became a ghost in their world, invisible and out of place. Then the orb the merchant had given me provided some kind of shield; as I noticed that the glowing-eyed figures who occasionally scanned their surroundings would overlook me entirely, their gazes sliding past as if I didn't exist.

But the isolation was unbearable. Because I was surrounded by billions of people, but yet I had never felt more alone. Then one night—or what I assumed was a night—I stood at the edge of a platform overlooking the city. And the view was breathtaking, and a endless expanse of light and motion. Then for a moment, I let myself wonder if this was my new reality. If I was stuck here, doomed to wander a future I couldn't begin to understand. But deep down, I knew I couldn't give up. And somewhere, somehow, my tether was still out there I just had to find it. So I closed my eyes and focused, and the orb in my hand pulsing faintly as if in response. Then the hum of the city faded, replaced by the sound of my own heartbeat. And slowly, faintly, I felt it—the familiar pull of the tether, like a faint pulse in the distance and it wasn't gone after all. So I opened my eyes, determination hardening in my chest. And I didn't know how long it would take or what I'd have to do, but I would find my way back because I had to.

Then the days—or what felt like days—had passed, and I was still here, wandering the city of Solara. At first, and the awe of it all kept me moving. And I couldn't stop staring at the floating streets, or the ever-shifting buildings, and the people whose very existence seemed more advanced than I could comprehend. But the awe quickly gave way to frustration because I wasn't just lost in this world. I was completely out of my depth. Because even the most mundane aspects of their society were overwhelming. And their "markets" didn't use currency in any way I understood. Transactions were conducted with gestures, holograms, and glowing symbols that floated in the air before vanishing into the ether. Then there were no stores or stalls in the way I recognized, just platforms that materialized objects on demand.

And at first, I tried to mimic the locals, watching how they interacted with these platforms. But every time I tried, nothing happened. Then the platforms didn't respond to me. It was as if the entire system recognized that I didn't belong and refused to acknowledge my existence. Then the orb I'd been given by the merchant was the only thing keeping me grounded. And it pulsed faintly in my hand, with its glow warm and reassuring. But I had no idea how it worked or what it was protecting me from, but I didn't let it out of my sight.

Then the people—or beings, because I wasn't sure what to call them—continued to ignore me. And they moved with a purpose that I couldn't understand, and their glowing eyes fixed on something just beyond my perception. And occasionally, I'd catch snippets of their conversations—if you could call them that. And their words weren't spoken aloud but transmitted through flashes of light and faint vibrations in the air and still I was completely alone.

Then one night, or what I assumed was a night based on the dimming of the city's lights, I wandered into a quieter part of Solara. And the towering buildings here were fewer, and the streets were almost deserted. I stopped in front of what looked like a massive mural—except it wasn't a mural at all. And it was a projection, a living, breathing depiction of Earth's history. So I watched, mesmerized, as images of ancient civilizations, wars, technological advancements, and space exploration unfolded before me. Then the mural transitioned seamlessly from one era to the next, showing humanity's progress—and its failures. But then, the images stopped and the projection flickered, and a single word appeared in glowing symbols: "Extinction." Then my stomach twisted as the mural showed what had happened to Earth. Wars, climate collapse, pandemics—everything

16

spiraled into chaos until humanity was brought to the brink of annihilation. "Is this what happens to us?" I whispered, with my voice trembling. Then as if in response, the projection shifted to the year 3025 and read the current year then I thought to myself I'm in 3025 1,000 years from my time. And the Earth was still alive, but it was a shell of what it had once been. And the people I'd been seeing weren't entirely human anymore and they were hybrids, with their biology merged with technology in ways I couldn't fully comprehend and then I hoped that this was not my timeline like the person told me when I first arrived because this wasn't just an advanced alien society—it was a post-human one.

Then I staggered back, with my mind racing. What did this mean for me? For my timeline? Was this my future, or was I in an alternate reality entirely? Then my thoughts were interrupted by a faint hum behind me. And I turned to see a figure approaching—tall, with glowing silver eyes and skin that shimmered like liquid metal. Then they wore a flowing robe that seemed to ripple with light, and their presence made the air around me vibrate. "You're not one of us," they said, with their voice melodic but laced with something I couldn't identify. Then I gripped the orb tightly, and my heart pounding. "No. I'm not. I... I don't even know how I got here." Then the figure tilted their head, studying me with an intensity that made my skin crawl. "You're an anomaly. A relic from the past." "A relic?" I repeated, the word stinging more than I expected. "I'm just... I'm trying to get back home." Then the figure's gaze softened slightly. "Home no longer exists in the way you remember it and the timeline is fractured and now you are caught between 2 worlds."

"Fractured?" I asked, as desperation crept into my voice. "What does that mean? And how do I fix it?"
But they didn't answer right away. And instead, they reached out, with their fingers brushing against the orb in my hand. And it pulsed brighter at their touch, and the warmth intensifying. "This will protect you," they said, their tone cryptic. "But it cannot guide you. That is something only you can do." "Guide me? To where?" Then the figure stepped back, as their form began to blur. "You must find the Nexus it is the key to realigning your tether. Without it, you will drift off in time forever."

"The Nexus?" I shouted as they faded into the air, their form dissolving like mist. "Wait! Where is it? How do I find it?" But they were gone, and I was left standing in a empty street, and the orb glowing faintly in my hand.
The Nexus The Nexus the word repeated itself in my mind, echoing like a mantra and it was my only lead, my only chance at getting back to where I belonged. But I had no idea where to start or what I was even looking for. Then as I stared out at the city, its lights twinkling like artificial stars, Then I realized one thing: I

couldn't give up. I know that the future was strange, terrifying, and overwhelming, but I had to find my way through it and I had to find the Nexus.

(Medieval Europe)

Then the pull came again and this time, it was violent and not the gentle tugging I'd felt before, but a full-force rip that left me gasping as I was yanked through a vortex of swirling colors and faint echoes. Then I clutched the orb tightly, my only anchor to sanity as the world dissolved and reshaped itself around me. Then when I finally landed, the impact was jarring. And I hit the ground hard, and the wind knocked out of me. Then for a moment, all I could do was lie there, staring up at a dull, gray sky and the air smelled different—earthy, damp, and faintly metallic. So I sat up slowly, with my muscles aching. And around me was a sprawling field, dotted with patches of wildflowers and bordered by a dense forest. And in the distance, the silhouette of a massive stone castle rose against the horizon, and its turrets piercing the sky like jagged teeth.

I wasn't in Solara anymore then a chill in the air told me I was far from the future's technological warmth. As my clothes, modern and nondescript, looked out of place against the medieval backdrop. Then I brushed dirt off my jeans and took a cautious step forward, trying to make sense of where—or when—I was. Then the first sign of civilization came in the form of a dirt road winding through the field. So I followed it, and my heartbeat steady but cautious. And as I crested a hill, I saw it—a small village, nestled at the base of the castle. Smoke rose from chimneys, and I could hear the faint sound of voices, laughter, and the clanging of metal.

"Medieval Europe," I muttered under my breath. Then the realization hit me like a ton of bricks. I wasn't just out of my time; I was centuries, maybe even a millennium, away from anything familiar. Then as I approached the village, the details became clearer. Thatched-roof cottages lined the dirt streets, with their walls patched and weathered. And women in coarse linen dresses carried baskets of vegetables, while children ran barefoot, with their laughter echoing through the air. And a blacksmith worked at his forge, with the rhythmic clang of his hammer filling the street. So I tried to blend in, but my clothes immediately set me apart. People stopped what they were doing to stare at me, with their eyes wide with suspicion—and fear.

"Who are you?" a gruff voice demanded. Then I turned to see a burly man with a thick beard, holding an axe in one hand. "I'm... uh, a traveler," I stammered, trying to sound confident. "A traveler?" Then he eyed my clothes with a mix of curiosity and distrust. "From where?" Then I hesitated. Because what was I supposed to say? That I was from the 21st century and had somehow been teleported into their world? Because then they'd think I was insane—or worse, a witch. So then I responded "From far away,", keeping my tone vague. "I've been... lost for a long time." Then the man's eyes narrowed, but before he could press

19

further, an older woman stepped forward. And she had kind eyes and wore a simple woolen shawl. "Leave him be, Ulric. The boy looks like he's been through enough."

Then Ulric grunted but backed off, muttering something under his breath. "Thank you," I said to the woman, genuinely relieved. Then she nodded, with her gaze softening. "You'll need food and shelter. Come with me." So I followed her to her cottage, and a modest structure with a thatched roof with a small garden out front was in front of me. And inside, it was warm and cozy, and the air filled with the scent of stew bubbling over a fire. "What's your name?" she asked as she ladled the stew into a wooden bowl. "Michael," I said, taking a seat at the rough-hewn table "I'm Elspeth," she said, placing the bowl in front of me. "Eat. You look like you haven't had a proper meal in days." Then she wasn't wrong. I hadn't eaten anything substantial since I'd left my own timeline. The stew was simple—just vegetables and a bit of meat—but it was the best thing I'd tasted in weeks.

Then over the next few days—or weeks, time was hard to track—so I stayed in the village, trying to adapt to life in Medieval Europe. And Elspeth was a kind woman, treating me like a lost son or something, but the rest of the villagers remained wary of me. So I quickly learned that survival here wasn't easy. The days were long, filled with hard labor, and the nights were cold and dark. And there was no electricity, no running water, and no modern conveniences. And even the smallest tasks, like fetching water or starting a fire, were exhausting. But the hardest part was the constant threat of danger. And the villagers spoke in hushed tones about bandits roaming the countryside, raiding parties from rival lords, and even rumors of witchcraft.

Then one evening, as I sat by the fire in Elspeth's cottage, she told me about the castle. "That's the seat of Lord Aldred," she said, with her voice low. "He rules these lands—and the people in them—with an iron fist. So it's best to stay out of his sight." "Why?" I asked, my curiosity piqued. "Because he doesn't take kindly to strangers," she said simply. "Especially those who don't belong." And I didn't ask her to elaborate because I didn't need to.

Then as the days turned into weeks, I began to wonder if I'd ever leave this place. Then the tether I'd felt in Solara, faint and distant, was gone and I was stuck yet again, and fully immersed into a world that I didn't understand, with no way of knowing how to get back home. And every night, I clutched the orb tightly, hoping it would somehow guide me. But it remained silent, and its glow faint and steady. Then the villagers began to accept me, but only reluctantly. And I helped with chores, repaired fences, and even learned how to handle a horse. But no matter how much I adapted, I couldn't shake the feeling that I didn't belong.

Then a call to action came in the dead of night. As I was lying on the straw mattress in Elspeth's cottage, staring at the wooden beams of the ceiling, when I heard the sound of horses galloping through the village. Then shouts came next—urgent, panicked voices tearing through the silence. "Elspeth!" I called, bolting upright. And she was already at the door, peering out cautiously. "Soldiers," she whispered, her voice trembling. Then I joined her, pressing my face to the rough wood of the doorframe. Then the sight outside sent a chill down my spine. And men in steel armor, with bearing the emblem of Lord Aldred's crest—a snarling wolf—were storming through the village. As they carried torches, then the flames casting eerie shadows on the walls of the cottages.

"They're looking for someone," Elspeth said, with her voice tight. But I didn't need to ask who. Because for weeks, I had kept a low profile, but the villagers' whispers had a way of traveling. And my strange clothes, my odd habits—it was only a matter of time before someone mentioned me to the wrong person. "What do they want?" I asked, trying to keep the fear out of my voice. "To make an example," she replied grimly. "That's how he keeps control." Then before I could respond the door burst open, and two soldiers stormed in. "There he is!" one of them barked, pointing at me. Then I froze, as my heart pounded. "You're coming with us," the other soldier said, grabbing my arm roughly. Then I struggled, but they were stronger. Then Elspeth shouted, trying to intervene, but she was pushed aside. So as they dragged me out into the cold night, the villagers watched from the shadows, their faces etched with fear and guilt. And no one dared to intervene. Then the soldiers took me to the castle, where I was thrown into a damp, dark cell. And the walls were made of cold stone, and the only light came from a small, barred window high above.

Then for hours—maybe days—I sat there, as my mind raced and I knew I had to find a way out. Then it was during this time that I met them—the rebels. And they were led by a man named Cedric, a former knight who had turned against Lord Aldred after witnessing the atrocities he had committed. "We've heard about you," Cedric said when they brought me to their hidden camp in the forest. "The stranger who appeared out of nowhere." "I didn't ask to be here," I said, meeting his gaze. "I just want to go home." Then he studied me for a long moment before nodding. "We can help each other and if you fight with us, I'll do what I can to help you find your way back." It wasn't much of a choice. So I agreed.

Then the next few weeks were a whirlwind of training, planning, and skirmishes. And Cedric taught me how to wield a sword—though I wasn't great at it—and how to use a bow. And the rebels were few in number but resourceful, relying on guerrilla tactics to weaken Aldred's forces. Then I learned quickly that this wasn't just a fight for power and the peasants were starving, taxed into oblivion, and punished mercilessly for the smallest infractions. As Aldred's rule was a reign of terror, and the villagers were desperate for change. Then I found myself growing attached to the rebels, despite knowing my time here was temporary. And there was Aelric, a wiry young man with a sharp wit who always found a way to lighten up the mood; and Freya, a fierce warrior who had lost her family to Aldred's soldiers; then Margot, a healer whose gentle hands belied her fiery determination.

Then one night, as we sat around a campfire, Cedric laid out the plan. "We strike at dawn," he said, with his voice firm. "The castle gates will be lightly guarded. If we can breach them, we can take the keep and force Aldred to surrender." And it sounded simple enough, but I knew it would be anything but. So when dawn came, we moved under the cover of fog. Then the rebels were silent as shadows, and their movements precise and practiced. And my heart pounded in my chest as we approached the castle gates.

Then the first clash was chaotic. As arrows flew, swords clashed, and the air was filled with the sounds of battle. So I stayed close to Cedric, using my limited skills to hold my own. Then as we fought our way into the keep, where Aldred's soldiers made their last stand. The corridors were narrow, forcing us to fight hand-to-hand. Then finally, we reached the throne room. And Aldred was there, seated on a massive wooden throne, flanked by his remaining guards. And he was a large man, with his face twisted into a sneer. "So, this is the rabble that dares to challenge me," he said, with his voice dripping with contempt. Then Cedric stepped forward. "Your reign is over, Aldred. Surrender, and we'll show mercy." Then Aldred laughed, a deep, menacing sound. "Mercy? You think you can defeat me?" Then the final battle was brutal. As Aldred was a skilled fighter, and his guards were relentless. But we were determined.

And in the end, it was Cedric who struck the final blow, his sword piercing Aldred's chest. Then the tyrant fell to the ground, with his sneer replaced by a look of shock. Then when it was over, the rebels cheered, their voices echoing through the castle. So I stood there, bloodied and exhausted, feeling a mix of triumph and sorrow. And I had helped these people win their freedom, but I still didn't know how to find mine. Then that night, as we celebrated around a roaring fire, Cedric approached me. "You've earned your place among us," he said, clapping a hand on my shoulder. "Thank you," I said, with my voice quiet. "But I don't belong here." Then he nodded, understanding. "We'll help you however we can because you've done more for us than you know." Then as the celebration continued, I felt the now-familiar pull again. And I knew that my time in Medieval Europe was coming to an end. So I gripped the orb tightly, because I knew that it was time to move on.

(Periods of Enlightenment)

Then the pull happened again, and it was sharp and abrupt this time, like a lightning bolt through my core. And one moment I was celebrating with Cedric and the rebels, with my chest swelling with the exhilaration of victory. Then the next, I was tumbling through the void again, with my senses overwhelmed by swirling light and deafening silence. Then when I landed, it was far gentler than before as my feet touched cobblestones instead of dirt, and the crisp scent of ink, paper, and fresh bread filled the air. Then I opened my eyes to find myself in a bustling city square, and the architecture around me was strikingly different from the castles and cottages of Medieval Europe.

And the streets were lined with buildings of white stone, and their facades adorned with intricate carvings and pillars and people moved with a purposeful energy, while dressed in fine clothing that was far more refined than anything I had seen in centuries past. Because the men wore tailored coats and breeches, while the women glided past in flowing gowns adorned with lace and jewels. Then a towering statue caught my eye in the center of the square, its bronze surface gleaming in the sunlight and the plaque at its base read, "To the Enlightenment of Man, 1750." Then my breath hitched.

"The Age of Enlightenment," I whispered, then the realization sending a thrill down my spine. Then I wandered through the square, taking in the sights and sounds of this new era. And vendors shouted about their wares, from books to exotic spices, while street performers played string instruments that I didn't recognize but it felt...alive, vibrant, and brimming with intellectual energy. But it wasn't long before I found myself in a coffeehouse, drawn in by the tantalizing aroma and the animated chatter spilling out into the street. And inside, men gathered around tables covered in parchment, quills, and books, debating with fervor.

Then I took a seat near the back, trying to blend in. And the conversations around me were intense, touching on topics I had only ever read about—philosophy, science, politics, and the nature of existence itself. "What brings you here, stranger?" The voice startled me. Then I turned to see a man sitting across from me, his piercing blue eyes studying me with curiosity and he had a neatly trimmed beard and wore a simple yet elegant coat.
"I'm...just passing through," I said cautiously. Then he smiled, and his expression was warm and inviting. "This is a place for thinkers, not passersby. So tell me, what do you think of Voltaire's critique of the monarchy?" Then I blinked, caught off guard. "I...think he was right to challenge authority," I said, fumbling for words. "People deserve freedom, and rulers should be held accountable."

Then the man's smile widened. "Spoken like a true philosopher. I'm Jean-Jacques Rousseau." Then when he said that my jaw nearly dropped. Rousseau? One of the great minds of the Enlightenment I thought then I replied "I'm Michael,". "Michael," he repeated thoughtfully. "You have the air of someone with much to say. Perhaps you'd care to join our discussions?" Then for weeks— or what felt like weeks—I found myself immersed in the intellectual world of the Enlightenment era. And Rousseau introduced me to other great minds of the era, and each meeting was like stepping into a history book that came to life.

And there was Voltaire, sharp-tongued and quick-witted, who spoke with a passion that lit up any room he entered. And he loved challenging my views, and forcing me to think deeper than I ever had before. "What is freedom to you, Michael?" he asked one evening, leaning forward with a mischievous glint in his eye. "Freedom is...choice," I said after a moment. "The ability to determine your own path without interference." Then Voltaire nodded thoughtfully. "And yet, even with choice, man is often his own oppressor."

Then there was Immanuel Kant, whose philosophical precision left me in awe as he spoke of morality, reason, and the boundaries of human knowledge, and his words weaving a tapestry of ideas that left my head spinning. "So Michael," he said one afternoon as we strolled through a library, "what do you believe is the source of enlightenment?" "Knowledge," I said instinctively. Then he nodded but added, "And the courage to use it." Then the days faded with lectures, debates, and late-night discussions over coffee and wine and I felt like a student at the feet of giants, soaking in their wisdom and challenging my own perceptions of the world.

But it wasn't just the Enlightenment thinkers of this time I encountered. Because in a moment that felt like an anomaly the tug came again and pulled me through the void then, I was introduced to minds even older—legends like Plato and Socrates. And I was led to a small, private gathering in an ornate study, where an older man with a calm demeanor greeted me and his presence radiated wisdom, and when he spoke, his voice was gentle yet commanding.

"Michael," he said, extending a hand. "I am Plato." I was stunned and didn't know how he knew my name, but still I barely managed to return the handshake as Plato and Socrates, sat together as though time and space meant nothing, and they engaged me in conversations that felt like riddles wrapped in revelations. "What is the essence of your journey?" Socrates asked one evening, and his penetrating gaze cutting through me. "To find my way home," I said, the words feeling inadequate even as they left my lips. Then he smiled faintly. "And what is home? A place? Or a state of being?" And their questions haunted me, and lingering in my mind but despite the intellectual richness of the Enlightenment, I couldn't shake the feeling of being untethered to my connection of my own time and, it felt like it was slipping away.

Then the pull of time had become almost familiar to me as it came again, and yet each new destination brought a fresh sense of disorientation. And this time, as the swirl of light and energy subsided, I found myself standing in a dimly lit workshop, as the air crackling with an almost electric energy. Then tall coils hummed with power, and blue sparks danced across copper wiring. And at the center of it all stood a man with piercing eyes and a mustache that seemed to belong to a different era entirely. Nikola Tesla I quickly noticed.

Then for a moment, he simply stared at me, with his expression caught between curiosity and calculation. "Fascinating," he finally murmured, stepping forward and circling me as if I were one of his experiments brought to life. "You do not belong here, do you?" Then I swallowed hard, trying to find the right words. "No, I... I'm a traveler. Through time." And instead of skepticism, his face lit up with enthusiasm. "Time itself! A most elusive force, yet one I have often speculated upon. Come, let us speak further." And just like that, I was drawn into the orbit of one of history's greatest minds.

Then over the following weeks, I found myself assisting Tesla in his experiments, though my contributions were more observational than technical. Then he spoke to me about energy—free energy for all humanity—about his dreams of a world interconnected by wireless communication, and ideas that I knew would one day come to pass, albeit not in the way he had envisioned though. And Tesla was relentless in his pursuit of knowledge. He worked long hours, often forgetting to eat or sleep, completely consumed by the infinite possibilities of the universe. I had read about his struggles, and his rivalries with Edison and others who sought to undermine his genius, but seeing it firsthand made it all the more tragic. Because he was a man decades ahead of his time, and yet, despite all he had accomplished, he would die penniless and largely unrecognized.

Then as time went on, I shared with him only vague insights about the future. And I told him that his legacy would not be forgotten, and that one day people would marvel at his genius. Then he simply smiled at that, as if it were of little consequence to him. "My work is for the future, whether I see it or not and that is enough." Then when the time pull came again, I felt an unusual resistance—as if Tesla himself was somehow interfering, holding me in place. "Time is but a river," he said, looking at me with an intensity that sent shivers down my spine. "And you, my friend, are adrift. But perhaps, if one knows how to read the currents, then one may guide the course." Then before I could ask what he meant, the world around me blurred, and I was swept away once more, leaving behind a man who had understood the mysteries of the universe in ways few ever would.

And the sensation was all too familiar now—the disorienting pull, the shift in gravity, and the strange distortion of light that signaled another journey through time and I had lost count of how many times this had happened, and how many worlds I had stepped into, but only to be whisked away before I could fully comprehend the experience. But this time, something felt different. Then as I stumbled forward, the ground beneath me felt solid, damp from a recent rain. And the air was thick with the scent of old wood and parchment, with a stark contrast to the metallic sterility of the future I had visited or the raw, untamed wilderness of the distant past. Then I found myself standing in what appeared to be a workshop, cluttered with peculiar instruments and papers strewn across wooden tables. And the flickering glow of candlelight danced on the walls, casting long shadows of gears and scientific instruments.

Then a man stood before me, hunched over a table, scribbling furiously with a quill on a parchment filled with sketches and calculations and his presence was commanding yet oddly familiar—the bespectacled eyes, the long hair tied back, and the air of a mind constantly in motion. Then I recognized him instantly. Benjamin Franklin.

Then he turned toward me, with eyes squinting as if trying to discern whether I was a figment of his imagination or another experiment gone awry. "You seem out of place, young man," he mused, his voice calm yet filled with curiosity. "And yet, something tells me you have knowledge beyond this century."

Then I hesitated before answering and I thought to myself that honesty would be the best choice in this particular situation just like with Nikola Tesla then I replied "You're right, Mr. Franklin. I am not from this time."

And his expression didn't change—no shock, no disbelief, just intrigue. Then he set down his quill and folded his hands in front of him. "Fascinating. And what year do you hail from?" "2025," I said, watching for his reaction.

Then his lips curled into a half-smile. "Two centuries ahead. A man of the future, standing in my humble workshop. So tell me, do my experiments lead to anything worthwhile?" Then I couldn't help but smile. "More than you could ever imagine. Your work with electricity changes the world" and that seemed to satisfy him, but he wasn't done questioning me. Then he gestured toward a peculiar device on his desk—one I recognized from history books but never expected to see firsthand. And it was a small metallic key that hung from a wire, suspended in mid-air. "You see, I have long suspected that time does not flow as we perceive it and like the electrical current I have attempted to harness, and perhaps time can be conducted, stored, or even redirected."

And his words sent a chill down my spine. Then he was on the verge of understanding something I had only recently begun to grasp myself. "You're right," I admitted. "Time isn't linear. It bends and shifts and I'm proof of that."

26

Then Franklin leaned forward, with his eyes gleaming with excitement. "Then tell me, traveler, what is the purpose of your journey? Do you move through time at will, or are you merely a passenger on an uncontrollable voyage?" And that question hit me harder than I expected but before I could answer, that familiar sensation—the tightening in my chest, the warping of reality—began once more. Then the workshop around me blurred, and Franklin's form fading like a candle extinguished in the wind and his final words echoed in my ears as I was pulled into the unknown again: "Remember, young man, the greatest discoveries are often accidents. Perhaps you are meant to uncover something even I could not."

Then as the world around me continued to dissolve, I realized that I wasn't just learning from these great minds—but I was becoming a part of their history. And yet, I knew my journey was far from over. Then unlike any pull before instead of the turbulent, chaotic whirlwind of colors and sounds, this transition was slower, almost meditative and it was as though the universe itself wanted me to be prepared for what was coming. Then when I opened my eyes, I found myself standing in a dimly lit room, and the air heavy with the scent of herbs and burning incense. As the walls were lined with shelves overflowing with books and scrolls, and a massive oak table at the center of the room was covered with celestial charts, an astrolabe, and vials of strange liquids.

Then the man sitting at the table turned to face me. With his piercing eyes that seemed to see right through me, and his long beard, streaked with gray, gave him an air of wisdom and mystery. "I've been expecting you," he said, with his voice calm but carrying an undeniable weight. Then I froze. "You...know me?" Then I thought to myself he must know me just like Plato knew me. Then he gestured to a chair across from him. "Sit, Michael." And the way he said my name sent a chill down my spine so I obeyed, lowering myself into the chair and trying to steady my racing thoughts.

"I am Michel de Nostredame," he said, studying me closely. "But you may know me as Nostradamus." Wow Nostradamus I thought and the name hit me like a thunderclap. Because one of history's most enigmatic figures, best known for his cryptic predictions that spanned centuries and yet here I was, sitting across from him in what appeared to be his study. "How...how do you know who I am?" I stammered. Then he smiled faintly. "The stars whisper many things to those who know how to listen and your arrival was foretold, though the details were unclear and you are not of this time, are you?" "No," I admitted, feeling the weight of his gaze. "I'm not." "Then you have much to tell, and much to learn," he said, leaning forward. "Shall we begin?"

Then for what felt like weeks, I remained in Nostradamus's world a realm of secrets and celestial wonders. Then he shared with me his methods, and explained how he used astrology, ancient texts, and his own intuition to craft his prophecies. Then one night, as we sat by a roaring fire, he laid out one of his famous quatrains and asked me to interpret it. "The blood of the just will be demanded of London, and Burnt by fire in the year '66, Then the ancient lady will fall from her high place, and many of the same sect will be killed." Then I stared at the words, and the cryptic nature of them making my head spin. "This...sounds like the Great Fire of London," I said cautiously. "It happened in 1666." Nostradamus nodded. "Indeed. But tell me, Michael, does foreknowledge change the path, or does it ensure its fulfillment?" Then I hesitated. "I don't know," I admitted. "Maybe it depends on the person. Some might use it to prepare, while others might become trapped by it."

Then he stroked his beard thoughtfully. "An insightful answer because the burden of prophecy is that it often reveals only shadows, leaving the interpreter to stumble in the dark." Then as the days passed, our conversations grew deeper. And Nostradamus questioned me about the world I came from—its technology, its leaders, and its conflicts. And at first, I hesitated, unsure of how much to reveal. But his curiosity was infectious, and soon I found myself describing airplanes, computers, and even space exploration.

"You humans have reached for the stars, then," he mused one evening as we gazed at the night sky. "Somewhat," I said, feeling a pang of homesickness. "But we're still struggling with the same problems—greed, war, inequality. And sometimes it feels like we haven't learned much at all." Then he turned to me, with his expression unreadable. "And yet, progress is a spiral, not a straight line. And each ascent is hard-won, and each descent holds lessons." Then one of the most memorable moments came when I asked him about the future—specifically, my own. "Can you see where I'm going?" I asked hesitantly, the orb clutched tightly in my hand. Then Nostradamus studied me for a long time before answering. "Your path is not fixed, Michael. It bends and twists like a river, shaped by choices both yours and others'. But one thing is certain: you are meant to touch many lives, as they, in turn, will shape yours." And his words stayed with me echoing in my mind as I continued to learn from him.

But as the weeks stretched on, I began to feel the familiar restlessness returning. Then I knew my time here was running out. Then one night, as I stood by the window of his study, watching the stars, Nostradamus joined me. "You're leaving soon," he said then I nodded. "yea I can feel it." Then he placed a hand on my shoulder. "Then let me leave you with this: the future is a tapestry, woven with threads of light and shadow. Seek the light, Michael, but do not fear the shadow. Both are needed to create the whole." Then before I could respond, the pull returned—stronger and this time it was almost violent. Then the world around me blurred, and Nostradamus's study dissolved into darkness as I hurtled through the void once more, and his words lingered in my mind, as a beacon of wisdom in the chaos.

(Industrial Revolution)

Then the pull this time felt heavier, and almost suffocating. Then when I landed, I was greeted by the cacophony of hissing steam, and clanking metal, and the distant rumble of machinery. And the air was thick with soot and the pungent scent of coal, and the world around me was shrouded in a gray haze. Then I found myself standing in the middle of a bustling city, and though it was unlike any I'd seen before. As chimneys jutted into the sky, spewing black smoke into the heavens, and rows of brick factories loomed over narrow cobblestone streets. And crowds of people moved briskly, and their faces weary and lined with grime.

The Industrial Revolution. I'd read about it in school, but nothing could have prepared me for the harsh reality of being here. "Oi! Watch where you're standing!" a gruff voice barked behind me. Then I turned to see a man pushing a cart piled high with coal, with his face and clothes blackened by soot. Then he gave me a glare before moving on, and his shoulders slumped under the weight of his load. Then the scene was surreal, as a stark contrast to the intellectual refinement of the Enlightenment. And here, it was raw, gritty, and relentlessly human. And the air buzzed with activity, and yet there was an underlying tension, and a palpable sense of struggle.

Then as I wandered through the city, I passed rows of tenement houses where families huddled together in squalor. And children with hollow eyes played in the dirt, and their laughter tinged with a kind of desperation. Then the disparity between the wealthy industrialists and the laboring masses was stark, and it gnawed at me. But it wasn't long before I stumbled upon a factory. And the sound of machinery was deafening as I stepped inside, my senses overwhelmed by the heat, and the noise, plus the smell of oil. And workers, men and women alike, toiled away at massive machines, with their movements mechanical and devoid of energy.

"What are you doing here?" a young woman hissed, grabbing my arm and pulling me aside. "I'm just...looking around," I said, startled by her urgency. Then her eyes narrowed, and she glanced around nervously. "Well, you'd best not let the overseer catch you because he's got no patience for loafers." And her words were a warning, but they also carried a hint of something else—a quiet defiance that intrigued me. "Do you work here?" I asked. Then she scoffed. "Doesn't everyone? Unless you're one of the lucky ones sitting in a mansion on the hill." And her bitterness was palpable, and I couldn't blame her then I asked. "What's your name?" "Clara," she said reluctantly. "Why do you care?" "I want to help," I said earnestly. Then she laughed, a harsh, humorless sound. "Help? Unless you can stop time or make the machines disappear, there's no help to be had here." But I wasn't deterred. Over the next few days, I followed Clara and got to know the workers. And their stories were heartbreaking—long hours, dangerous conditions, pitiful wages, and little hope of a better future.

Then one evening, Clara introduced me to a group of workers who were meeting in secret to discuss their grievances. And they huddled in a dimly lit cellar, with their voices hushed but filled with determination. "We can't keep going like this," one man said, slamming his fist on the table. "The factory owners sit in their fancy houses while we're breaking our backs just to survive." "We need to organize," Clara said, her voice firm. "If we stand together, they can't ignore us." Then I found myself swept up in their passion, and my own sense of justice ignited by their plight. And by using what little knowledge I had, I offered suggestions on how they could draft a list of demands and present them to the factory owners.

"Unity is your greatest strength," I told them. "If you can show them that you're serious, that you're willing to strike if necessary, they'll have to listen." Then the weeks that followed were a blur of clandestine meetings, late-night planning sessions, and tense negotiations. And the workers were scared but resolute, and their fear tempered by the hope of change. Then finally, the day of the strike arrived. And the factory floor was eerily quiet as the workers laid down their tools and marched out into the streets, and their voices rising in a chorus of demands.

"What's the meaning of this?" a portly man in a fine suit bellowed, and his face red with anger. "This is the meaning," Clara said, stepping forward. "We're tired of being treated like machines. We deserve fair wages, safer conditions, and basic respect." Then the man sneered. "You think you can intimidate me with your little parade? Get back to work, or you'll all be replaced by morning." But the workers stood firm, and their resolve unshaken and it was a tense standoff, as the air cracked with anticipation.

Then in the end, it wasn't the factory owner's heart that softened—it was the pressure from the public, who sympathized with the workers' plight. Then after weeks of negotiations, the workers won modest concessions—a small but significant victory. And as I stood among them, watching their faces light up with hope, I felt a profound sense of accomplishment. Then for the first time in what felt like forever, I had made a tangible difference I thought.

But the celebration was short-lived. And that familiar pull returned, tugging at me with a force I couldn't resist. "No," I whispered, and panic started rising in my chest. "Not yet." Then Clara noticed my distress. "What's wrong?" "I have to go," I said, my voice trembling. "But thank you...for everything." Then before she could respond, the world around me dissolved into a blur of light and sound, and I was hurtling through the void once more.

Then as I tumbled through time and space, Clara's voice echoed in my mind, a reminder of the resilience and strength of the human spirit. And the pull this time was harsher, tearing through me like a gale-force wind. Then when I finally landed, I was on familiar cobblestones, surrounded by the same sooty air and relentless grind of machinery. But something felt...off. The streets seemed busier, the factories even more numerous, and the faces in the crowds were different. And I was still in the Industrial Revolution—but it wasn't the same moment I had left. Because as I looked around, I realized it had been years since my first visit. I was three years ahead of where I'd been before. And the city had changed in subtle but significant ways. Because now there were new buildings, larger and more imposing, and casting even darker shadows over the narrow streets. And the crowds were thicker, and the noise of machinery was louder, and a deafening hum that seemed to permeate every corner of the city.

So I wandered aimlessly for a while, with my mind racing. Because what was I supposed to do here? And why had I been brought back? Then the answer came when I stumbled upon a group of workers gathered outside a factory, and their faces grim and determined. And they were holding signs, with their messages scrawled in bold letters: "FAIR WAGES NOW," "STOP CHILD LABOR," and "SAFETY OVER PROFITS." And this was no ordinary day it was the beginning of a strike. Then I edged closer, listening to their conversations. And their grievances were the same as before—low wages, long hours, and unsafe working conditions—but there was a new energy in the air, and a sense of desperation mingled with hope.

"They think they can silence us," a burly man said, with his voice tinged with anger. "But we've had enough. We're not backing down this time." "They'll call the authorities," a woman warned, her voice trembling. "We could be arrested—or worse." "Let them," the man shot back. "It's time we stood up for ourselves." Then I felt a tug of recognition as I watched them. And they reminded me of Clara and the workers I'd aided years ago. But Clara was nowhere to be seen. And this was a new group, facing the same old battle. And it didn't take long for me to make my decision.

Then I approached the group cautiously, introducing myself and offered to help. And at first, they were skeptical, but as I shared the strategies I'd learned during my previous visit their wariness of me began to fade.
"Who are you, really?" one of them asked, with his eyes narrowing. "You talk like you've done this before." "I've been...involved in similar struggles," I said carefully. It wasn't a lie, but I couldn't exactly tell them the truth. Then over the next few weeks, I became deeply involved in their cause. And I helped them organize their efforts, draft petitions, and coordinate their strikes and it wasn't easy—and there were countless setbacks, including threats from the factory owners and intimidation from hired thugs.

Then one night, as we huddled in a cramped basement planning our next move, an older worker named Ewan shared his story. "I've worked in that factory for twenty years," he said, and his voice thick with emotion. "Lost two fingers to the machines, and my lungs ain't been the same since the accident. But what choice do I have? It's work or starve." Then his words hit me like a punch to the gut. Because The Industrial Revolution wasn't just a period of innovation and progress—it was a time of immense human suffering, and people like Ewan bore the brunt of it. Then I found myself becoming more passionate, and more determined to help. Then when the factory owners refused to negotiate, I encouraged the workers to take their demands to the public, organizing rallies and distributing pamphlets. Then the rallies were electrifying as workers from other factories joined in, and their voices rising in a powerful chorus of unity. And the streets were alive with the sound of their chants, a defiant cry for justice that echoed through the city.

But the fight wasn't without its dangers. And on more than one occasion, the authorities tried to break up the rallies, by using brute force to disperse the crowds. And I narrowly avoided being arrested several times, while slipping away just as the police closed in. Then one particularly tense moment came when the factory owners hired a group of enforcers to intimidate the workers. And they showed up at one of our rallies, armed with clubs and ready to cause trouble. "Stand your ground," I told the workers, my voice steady despite the fear gnawing at me. "They want to scare us, but we can't let them win." Then the confrontation was intense, but the workers held firm, with their unity and resolve proving stronger than the enforcers' threats and it was a small victory, but it felt monumental.

Then as the weeks wore on, I found myself forming bonds with the workers, and their struggles and triumphs became my own. But there was always a nagging thought in the back of my mind—a reminder that I didn't belong here, and that I was living on borrowed time. Then one night, as I stood on a rooftop overlooking the city, Ewan joined me. "You've done a lot for us, Michael," he said, his voice filled with gratitude. "We couldn't have come this far without you." Then I looked at him, struggling to find the words. "I just want to help. That's all." Then he nodded, with his gaze fixed on the horizon. "Well, you've done more than help. You've given us hope." And his words warmed my heart, but they also made the inevitable departure even harder to bear. Then the pull came not long after, wrenching me away from the world I'd come to care about. And ass the factory-lined streets dissolved into darkness, I couldn't help but wonder if the workers would continue the fight without me—or if history would simply repeat itself.

(World War I)

Then the pull came again and was like a punch to the chest this time, and yanking me out of one reality and hurling me into another. And I landed hard, face-first in mud, as the sound of deafening explosions rattled in my eardrums. Then the ground beneath me trembled as though the earth itself was in agony and my hands instinctively dug into the muck as I tried to regain my bearings. Then when I looked up, I was met with chaos and soldiers in khaki uniforms scrambled around me, with their faces streaked with mud and fear. And trenches stretched endlessly in both directions, with their walls damp and crumbling. And overhead, the sky was a grim shade of gray, streaked with smoke from the constant barrage of artillery fire.

Then I noticed that I was in the middle of World War I. "Get down!" a soldier shouted, pulling me roughly by the arm. Then he threw me into a trench just as a shell exploded nearby, sending a shower of dirt and debris raining down. "What are you doing out in the open?" he barked, his face inches from mine. And he looked young, and barely older than me, but his eyes were hollow, and weighed down by horrors that I couldn't even begin to imagine. "I—I don't know," I stammered, struggling to come up with an excuse. "I got separated." I said and he didn't question it because there was no time so he handed me a rifle, and its weight unfamiliar and unsettling in my hands.

"Stay low," he said. "And for God's sake, keep moving." And I nodded, with my heart hammering in my chest. Then the trench was a labyrinth of narrow passageways, and packed with soldiers who moved with grim determination. And some were shouting orders, and others were tending to the wounded, with their makeshift bandages soaked with blood. And the air was thick with the acrid stench of gunpowder and the metallic tang of blood. And every step was a struggle, with my boots sinking into the muck that lined the bottom of the trench. As I could hear the distant rat-a-tat of machine guns, punctuated by the occasional scream.

"What the hell am I doing here?" I muttered under my breath. But there was no time for answers and before I could process the madness around me, an officer appeared, barking orders. "Prepare to go over the top!" he shouted. Then the soldiers around me groaned, with their faces pale but resigned and my stomach churned as I realized what he meant because we were going to charge. Then as we lined up at the base of the trench, the officer blew a whistle, signaling the attack and my legs felt like lead as I scrambled up the ladder, with my rifle clutched tightly in my hands. Then the world above was a nightmare and the battlefield was a hellscape of craters, barbed wire, and mangled bodies. And the sound of gunfire was deafening, and a relentless cacophony that made it impossible to think.

So I ran blindly, following the others as we charged toward the enemy lines while bullets whizzed past me, and some were so close I could feel the heat. So I threw myself into a crater, panting and shaking, with my mind racing with panic. "Move, damn it!" someone shouted, pulling me to my feet. As I stumbled forward, with my body acting on instinct. Then the rifle in my hands felt useless; and I had no idea how to aim or let alone fire it. But survival was all that mattered.

Then the next few weeks passed in a haze of terror and exhaustion. And I became one of them—a soldier in the trenches, fighting for survival in a war I didn't understand. And I learned to navigate the endless labyrinth of mud and barbed wire, to distinguish between the different types of artillery fire, and to keep my head down when the shells came too close. And there were moments of quiet, brief respites between the battles, but even then, the fear never left. And at night, I huddled in the trench with the others, and the distant sound of gunfire was a constant reminder of the war that never seemed to end. But I bonded with the soldiers around me, though I was careful not to reveal too much about myself. And they were a mix of hardened veterans and fresh-faced recruits, and each with their own stories of loss and longing.

Then one night, as we sat around a small fire, a soldier named Tom shared his story.
"Got a wife back home," he said, his voice soft and wistful. "She's expecting our first child. A boy, I hope."
Then others nodded, murmuring their own hopes and dreams. And for a moment, the war seemed distant, like a shadow on the edge of our thoughts. But that moment never lasted. And the war always came back, dragging us into its relentless grasp. And I fought alongside them, with my survival instincts kicking in despite my lack of training. But I learned to fire the rifle, to throw grenades, and to crawl through the mud under enemy fire. And each day felt like a lifetime, with each battle a test of my will to live.

But there were moments of humanity amidst the horror. And I helped a wounded soldier reach the medics, carrying him on my back through a hail of bullets. And as I shared my rations with a young recruit who hadn't eaten in days. I listened to the stories of men who had lost everything, offering what little comfort I could. And Still, the war took its toll on me. And I saw friends fall, with their lifeless bodies as a stark reminder of how fragile life was. And I endured the constant fear, and the gnawing hunger, as the bone-deep exhaustion. And through it all, I kept asking myself the same question: Why am I here? Then the answer came one fateful day when I found myself in the midst of a brutal battle. And the enemy had launched a surprise attack, and we were outnumbered and outgunned.

But as chaos erupted around me, I saw Tom pinned down by enemy fire, and his leg bleeding profusely. And without thinking, I ran to him, dragging him to safety and even as bullets rained down.

"Why did you do that?" he asked, with his voice weak but grateful. "Because someone has to," I said, with my voice trembling. And in that moment, I realized why I had been brought here. And it wasn't about winning the war or changing the course of history—it was about making a difference, but however small, in the lives of those around me. Then as the days turned into weeks, I continued to fight, to survive, to help wherever I could. But I knew it couldn't last. Then the pull would come eventually, and tearing me away from this place and these people. Then when it finally came, I felt a pang of sadness. And I had grown to care for the soldiers, and their struggles and sacrifices etched into my heart. Then as the world dissolved around me, I whispered a silent prayer for them—for their courage, their humanity, and their hope in the face of unimaginable darkness.

And the transition was smoother this time—but less of a violent wrenching and more like sinking slowly into warm water. Then when I opened my eyes, the roar of artillery and the chaos of war were gone. And in their place was an eerie stillness, and the quiet that follows a storm. Then I was standing in the middle of a cobblestone street, and it was lined with brick buildings that bore the scars of battle. And windows were shattered, and some structures leaned precariously, as if they might collapse at any moment. And it was 1919, the year after World War I, but the world still felt broken. And the air was thick with the smell of damp earth and coal smoke, and the people I saw moved with a heaviness, with their eyes downcast and their faces gaunt. And they weren't just survivors—they were ghosts, haunted by memories they couldn't escape.

Then as I took in my surroundings, I noticed a figure sitting on the steps of a crumbling building. And he was slouched forward, with a cigarette dangling from his lips, and his uniform jacket hanging loosely on his thin frame. And it was Tom. Then I froze, and my heart leaping into my throat because he looked older, and more worn, but there was no mistaking him. And he was definitely one of the soldiers that I had fought alongside, and the one that I had dragged to safety during one of the war's bloodiest battles.

So I approached him cautiously, and unsure if he would even recognize me. "Tom?" I said softly. Then His head snapped up, with his bloodshot eyes narrowing as he studied me. Then for a moment, there was no recognition, just a flicker of suspicion. Then his expression softened. "Michael?" he said, with his voice hoarse. "I thought you were dead." Then I smiled faintly, sitting down beside him. "Not quite but how are you holding up?" Then he let out a bitter laugh, taking a long drag of his cigarette. "How do you think?" he responded as we sat in silence for a while, and the weight of everything unsaid hanging between us. Then finally, he spoke. "War's over, but it doesn't feel like it," he muttered. "Because every night, I hear the guns and see their faces. And every day, I wake up and wonder why it wasn't me."

Then I glanced at him, and my chest tightening as he looked like a man on the edge, teetering between despair and something even darker. "What can I do to help?" I asked. Then he laughed again, with a hollow sound. "Unless you can turn back time, there's nothing anyone can do." But I refused to accept that. And over the next few days, I stayed by his side, determined to pull him out of the darkness. And it wasn't easy and he was angry, bitter, and drowning in a sea of guilt and regret. Then one night, I found him in an alley, slumped against the wall with a bottle of whiskey in one hand and a syringe in the other. Then my heart sank as I realized what he was about to do.

"Tom," I said sharply, snatching the syringe from his hand. "What the hell are you doing?" Then he looked up at me, and his eyes filled with tears. "I can't take it anymore, Michael. The nightmares, the pain...it's too much." Then I knelt beside him, gripping his shoulders. "I know it's hard. But this isn't the answer. You survived the war, Tom. Don't let it take you now." Then he broke down, sobbing into his hands. And it was the first time That I had seen him show any emotion other than anger or indifference.

Then from that moment on, I made it my mission to help him heal. And I found him in a room in a boarding house, then I cleaned him up, and got him something to eat. And I listened as he poured out his pain, his guilt over the friends he had lost, and his struggle to find purpose in a world that no longer made sense. But it wasn't enough. Then the addiction had its claws in him, and breaking free was a constant battle. And I stayed up with him through the sleepless nights, holding him as he shook from withdrawal and reassuring him when the cravings became unbearable. And at times, it felt hopeless. And there were days when he lashed out, accusing me of meddling, of not understanding what he was going through. But I refused to give up on him.

But slowly, he began to improve. And he started eating regularly, gaining back some of the weight he had lost. And he found a job at a local factory, and the routine gave him a sense of stability. And most importantly, he began to believe in himself again. Then one evening, as we sat on the steps of his boarding house, he turned to me with a faint smile. "I don't know how to thank you, Michael," he said. "I wouldn't be here if it weren't for you."
"You don't have to thank me," I said. "You're the one who fought to get better. I just gave you a little push." Then he nodded, and his expression thoughtful.
"You're a good man, Michael. I hope you find whatever it is you're looking for." And his words stayed with me long after I left. Then when the pull finally came, taking me away from 1919 and back into the unknown, I felt a strange sense of

peace even though I hadn't been able to save everyone I had saved Tom. And sometimes, that was enough.

(The Jazz Era)

And the pull this time was strange, but less of a violent tug and more like a gentle invitation. Then when I opened my eyes, I was standing on a bustling city street, and the air alive with music, laughter, and the hum of an era that seemed to be on the brink of something extraordinary. And bright electric lights illuminated the scene, with their glow spilling onto the cobblestones below. And men in sharp suits and women in flowing dresses and feathered headpieces strolled past me, with their steps in sync with the rhythm of a distant jazz band.

Then I noticed that I was in the 1920s. The Jazz Age. And the street seemed to pulse with energy, with every corner alive with something new. And automobiles clattered down the road, and their horns adding to the chaotic symphony of the night as speakeasies thrived behind unmarked doors, and their entrances guarded by men who looked as though they'd seen more than their fair share of trouble. Then I walked cautiously, taking in my surroundings. And a marquee caught my eye, with its bold letters announcing a performance by none other than Louis Armstrong. Then my heart raced because I had read about him, and about this time when jazz redefined music and gave a voice to a generation.

Then the sound of a trumpet pierced the air, and its melody raw and jubilant, pulling me toward a small club tucked between towering buildings and the place was packed, with bodies swaying in unison, and their movements as fluid as the music. Then I slipped inside, feeling the heat of the room immediately. Then the band on stage played with a fervor that I had never experienced before. Then the trumpet player—Louis himself—commanded the space, with his notes soaring, and his eyes alive with passion. Then the crowd roared and its approval as he launched into another tune, with his fingers dancing over the keys of his instrument. I found myself drawn into the rhythm, with my foot tapping, and my body swaying despite myself.

"This is the place to be, huh?" a voice said beside me. Then I turned to see a young man grinning at me, with his suspenders loose over a crisp white shirt. "It's incredible," I said, with my voice barely audible over the music. Then he chuckled. "First time in a jazz club? You've got that look about you." "Something like that," I said, trying to hide my amazement. Then we talked for a while, shouting over the music, and I learned his name was Henry. And he was a writer, a dreamer, and someone chasing the American Dream in a time when it felt like anything was possible.

Then the weeks blurred together and then the tug threw me some more years forward, and each night brought something new—a different club, a new band, or another encounter with the wild, unrelenting energy of the Jazz Age. Then I became a regular at the speakeasies, slipping past secret entrances and soaking in the music and the stories of those who lived for these moments of rebellion and joy. But it wasn't all glamour. Then one night, as I walked home from a particularly lively performance, I noticed a man slumped against a brick wall, with his face pale and his clothes tattered. And his eyes were sunken, with his hands trembling.

"Hey, are you alright?" I asked, kneeling beside him. Then he looked at me, with his expression hollow. "Lost it all in the crash," he said. "Stocks, savings...everything." And then The Great Depression was beginning to cast its shadow and it was a stark contrast to the vibrant scenes that I had grown accustomed to. And as the days passed, I began to notice the cracks in the façade of prosperity. And breadlines formed on street corners, and their lines stretched endlessly with men in suits, and their faces etched with despair, wandered aimlessly, clutching newspapers that screamed of economic ruin.

And even the jazz clubs, once bursting with life, began to feel the strain. As the crowds thinned, their laughter quieter, and their steps slower. Then one night, Henry found me at a near-empty bar. And he looked different, with his carefree demeanor replaced with a somber weight. "I got laid off," he said, staring into his drink. "Boss said they can't afford to keep everyone. Guess I wasn't 'essential.'" I didn't know what to say. I wanted to comfort him, to tell him things would get better, but I didn't know if that was true. Then we sat in silence for a while, and the music from the band a faint echo of the energy it once held. "This city, this world," Henry said finally. "It chews you up and spits you out, doesn't it?" "It doesn't have to," I said, my voice firm. "You're more than this moment, Henry. You'll find a way." Then he looked at me, with his eyes searching mine. "You really believe that?" Then I nodded, though I wasn't sure if I was trying to convince him or myself.

Then as the weeks stretched on, I did what I could to help those around me. And I volunteered at soup kitchens, and handed out spare change to those who needed it, and I offered words of encouragement to those who had lost hope and it wasn't much, but it was something. Then I realized that The Jass Age wasn't just about the music or the parties because it was also about resilience. And it was about finding joy in the face of hardship, and about creating something beautiful even when the world was falling apart. Then when the pull came, I felt a pang of sadness because I had grown to love this time, despite its struggles. And the people, the music, and the spirit of survival—was something I would carry with me forever. Then as the world dissolved around me, I whispered a silent goodbye to the 1920s & 30s, to Henry, and to the music that had filled my soul and reminded me of the power of hope.

Then the transition hit me harder this time, as if my very essence was being shoved into a new time and place with no regard for my physical or mental state. Then when I opened my eyes, I was standing in the middle of a street so quiet it felt eerie. Then the energy of The Jazz Era was gone. And the lively jazz, the parties, the carefree nights—they had all faded into a bleak, oppressive silence. Then I glanced around, and the scene before me a stark contrast to the vibrant streets that I had walked not long ago. And the buildings looked the same, but the spirit had vanished. And now the signs of the Great Depression was everywhere—boarded-up storefronts, long lines of weary people waiting outside soup kitchens, and faces that wore the weight of too many hardships.

Then I walked down the street, with my shoes crunching on the frosted ground because winter had come, and it seemed to amplify the desolation. And families huddled together on the steps of buildings, with their clothes worn and patched, and their eyes hollow. And this was the end of the 1930s, and it felt like the world was holding its breath, waiting for something—anything—to change. Then I wandered aimlessly until I found myself at a public square where a small crowd had gathered. Then a man in a tattered overcoat stood atop of a makeshift stage, with his voice hoarse but filled with determination.

"We can't give up!" he shouted, his breath visible in the frigid air. "This isn't the end! We've survived wars, plagues, and disasters and we'll survive this too!" Then the crowd murmured in response, and some nodding while others looked away too tired or too broken to believe him. Then I stayed to listen, captivated by his words. And he spoke of hope, of resilience, of rebuilding. And as I watched the crowd, I realized something: despite the despair, there was still a spark of life, a flicker of resistance. Then after the speech ended, I approached the man as he stepped down from the platform. "Strong words," I said, offering him a small smile. Then he looked at me, with his face gaunt but his eyes sharp. "Words are all we have left," he replied. "If we lose hope, we lose everything." Then we fell into conversation, and I learned his name was Robert. And he had once been a successful businessman, but the crash had taken everything—his company, his home, and nearly his family. But yet here he was, rallying others, refusing to let despair win.

Then I spent the next few weeks following Robert and others like him, and people who refused to let the weight of the Depression crush their spirits. So I helped in small ways—distributing food at soup kitchens, fixing broken windows in abandoned buildings turned into shelters, and also lending a listening ear to those who needed it. Then one day, Robert introduced me to a young woman named Amy. And she ran a small community center that had somehow managed to survive the economic collapse. And it was a beacon of hope in an otherwise bleak world, that was offering free meals, warm clothing, and a place for people to gather and share their stories. And Amy was a force of nature and she moved through the center with a purpose, with her voice calm and steady as she reassured the people around her.

"We'll get through this," she said to an elderly man who clutched a threadbare coat. "It won't always be this hard." And I couldn't help but admire her because she had lost her husband and her home, but yet she poured every ounce of her strength into helping others. Then one evening, as we worked side by side organizing donations, she turned to me and said, "Why do you do it? You don't look like someone who's been hit hard by the Depression." Then I hesitated, unsure how to explain. "I guess I just want to help," I said finally. "It feels...important." Then she studied me for a moment, and then nodded. "Well, you're good at it. People need someone to believe in." And her words stayed with me. In a world that seemed determined to break everyone, and the simple act of believing—of holding onto hope—felt like an act of defiance.

Then as the days passed, I saw small signs of change. And a group of men banded together to repair a bridge that had been damaged in a storm. While a family opened their home to strangers, offering what little they had to those who had less. And the spirit of the community began to stir, like embers reigniting after a long, cold night. But it wasn't all progress. And there were moments of anger, of frustration, of despair and even fights broke out over scraps of food, and some people gave up entirely, disappearing into the shadows. Then one night, as I walked through the city, I stumbled upon a young boy huddled in an alley, with his face pale and his hands trembling from the cold.

"Hey," I said softly, kneeling beside him. "Are you alright?" Then he shook his head, and his eyes filling with tears. "I'm hungry," he whispered. Then I wrapped my coat around him and carried him to Amy's community center, where she immediately took him in. And watching her tend to the boy, with her face gentle and her hands steady, I felt a surge of gratitude because for all the darkness, there were still people like Amy and Robert, and people who refused to give up, who found light in even the darkest times. Then when the pull finally came, I felt a bittersweet pang because I had grown attached to this time like all the others before it, and to these people who fought so hard to survive and to help one another. Then as the world around me dissolved, I whispered a silent promise to carry their resilience with me, no matter where—or when—I ended up next.

(World War 2)

So when the pull came suddenly again, it yanked me out of the haze of the Great Depression and thrusting me into a world I was completely unprepared for. And my body hit the ground hard, with the impact jarring me to my core. Then my ears were ringing, and the world around me was a blur of chaos and noise. Then when I finally managed to lift my head the scene before me made my stomach drop because explosions lit up the night sky, and their fiery brilliance contrasting sharply with the inky darkness. As men in uniforms sprinted past me, and shouted orders I couldn't make out over the deafening roar of gunfire. And the acrid smell of smoke and gunpowder burned my nostrils, and the earth beneath me trembled with every nearby blast.

Then I noticed that I was in the middle of a warzone again and before I could process what was happening, a soldier grabbed my arm, and his face streaked with dirt and sweat. "Get up!" he shouted, his voice barely audible over the chaos. "Move, now!" Then my instinct took over, and I scrambled to my feet, following him and as he led me toward a trench we dove in just as another explosion rocked the ground behind us. "What the hell are you doing out there?" he demanded, with his eyes scanning me with a mix of confusion and irritation. "I...I got lost," I stammered, unsure of how else to explain my sudden appearance. "Lost? In the middle of a goddamn battlefield?" he scoffed. "You're lucky you didn't get blown to bits." Then he handed me a rifle with the cold metal foreign and heavy in my hands. "You know how to use this?" then I shook my head, and he muttered a curse under his breath. "Stay low, keep your head down, and for God's sake, don't shoot me."

Then before I could respond, he was gone, and climbing out of the trench and disappearing into the chaos above. And I stayed where I was, with my heart pounding as I tried to make sense of my surroundings because I had read about World War 2 in history books, and seen the black-and-white photos of soldiers and battlefields, but nothing could have prepared me for the raw, visceral reality of being here and plus the air was thick with fear and desperation, and every sound a reminder that death was just a heartbeat away. Then for weeks, I was thrown into the thick of it, moving from one battle to the next alongside men who had become my comrades. Then there he was Henry, the sharp-tongued rifleman from Brooklyn who always seemed to find a joke even in the darkest moments. Then there was Paul, the quiet, steady medic who carried the weight of every life he couldn't save.

And we fought together, ate together, and slept in shifts, always wary of the next attack. Then the days blurred into one another, and it was a relentless cycle of violence and exhaustion. Then one night, as we huddled around a small fire in the ruins of a bombed-out village, Henry turned to me. "You don't talk much about where you're from," he said, with his voice low. Then I hesitated. "Because it doesn't feel important right now." Then Paul glanced at me, with his expression thoughtful. "And it's all we've got out here—where we've been, who we are and it keeps us human." And I didn't know how to explain my situation, so I settled for half-truths. "I'm from New York. Grew up in the city." Then Henry grinned. "Brooklyn's better." Then I chuckled despite myself, grateful for the brief moment of levity. But the war didn't allow for many of those moments.

Then one morning, we were ambushed while crossing an open field. Then a sudden burst of gunfire sent us diving for cover, and the air filled with shouts and screams. "Michael, move!" Henry shouted, with his voice cutting through the chaos. And I scrambled to my feet, with my adrenaline coursing through me as I followed him toward a cluster of trees with bullets whizzing past us, and each one a reminder of how fragile life was in this place. Then we made it to cover, but not everyone did. Then when the dust finally settled, I saw Paul lying motionless on the ground, with his uniform stained with blood. So I ran to him, dropping to my knees as I pressed my hands against his wound, desperate to stop the bleeding.

"Stay with me," I pleaded, as my voice Shaked. Then he opened his eyes, with his gaze unfocused. "It's alright," he whispered. "You did good, kid." Then he died moments later, and I felt something inside me break.
Then the weeks that followed were a blur of grief and determination and I fought harder, ran faster, and did everything I could to keep the rest of my comrades alive. But the war didn't care about my efforts and it was an unrelenting force, taking and taking until there was nothing left and by the time the pull came again, I was more than ready to leave. Then as the world around me dissolved, I whispered a silent prayer for Henry, for Paul, and for all the others who had given everything in a war that seemed endless.

Then the transition was subtle this time, and not the violent yank that I had grown accustomed to. And one moment, I was surrounded by the cacophony of war; then the next, I found myself standing on a quiet suburban street. And the air was still carrying the faint scent of freshly cut grass and blooming flowers. And the houses were modest, and each one with a neatly kept lawn, picket fences, and a sense of order that felt almost surreal after the chaos of World War 2.

Then it didn't take me long to realize that I was in America, somewhere in the 1950s and the cars parked along the street were boxy chrome grilles that gleamed in the sunlight. And kids rode bicycles, with their laughter ringing out as they raced down the sidewalk. And the world seemed at peace—and a stark contrast to the battlegrounds I had just left, But there was a heaviness in my chest, a lingering ache from the war that hadn't quite healed. And I thought of Paul, the medic who had been the quiet backbone of our unit. And his death had left a hole in our group and in me.

Then I walked aimlessly, and unsure of my purpose here, until I saw a woman standing on the porch of a small house and I noticed that she was hanging laundry on a line, and her movements were precise and methodical. And her face was familiar—too familiar because it was Paul's wife, Rose. Then I froze, with my breath catching in my throat. And I noticed that the years had aged her slightly, but her eyes still held the warmth and strength Paul used to talk about during quiet moments in the trenches.

Then driven by a pull I couldn't explain, I approached the house. And my footsteps crunched on the gravel driveway, catching her attention. Then she turned to me, with her expression wary but polite.
"Can I help you?" she asked, shielding her eyes from the sun. Then I hesitated, and the words got suck in my throat. Because how could I explain who I was and why I was here? "I...knew Paul," I said finally, with my voice soft. Then her eyes widened slightly, and she set down the laundry basket. "You served with him?" Then I nodded. "He was a good man. One of the best." Then she invited me inside, her demeanor cautious but kind. And the house was modest but cozy, and filled with the warmth of a family home and photographs lined the walls, and many of them of Paul in his uniform, and his smile as genuine as ever.

Then two children ran into the room, and their laughter filled the air. And a boy and a girl, both with Paul's features—and the same sharp eyes, with the same mischievous grin. And my heart clenched at the sight. "This is Michael," Rose said, introducing me to them. "He knew your father." Then the boy, who couldn't have been older than ten, stared at me with wide eyes. "Did you fight in the war with him?" Then I nodded. "We were in the same unit. And he was brave and kind, and always looking out for everyone." Then the girl, who was younger, clung to her mother's skirt, and her expression shy but curious.

Then over the next few weeks, I became a fixture in their lives. And I helped Rose with the household chores, and I fixed the broken fence in the backyard, and taught the kids how to throw a baseball and it was a stark departure from the battles and survival that I had become accustomed to, but it was exactly what I needed—a chance to give back to someone who had lost so much. Then Rose opened up to me slowly, sharing stories about her life with Paul. And she spoke of their love, their dreams, and the void his death had left behind. "I tried to be strong," she admitted one evening as we sat on the porch and the kids were asleep, and the stars shone brightly overhead. "For the kids, mostly. But some days, it feels impossible." "You've done more than most could," I said. "Paul would be proud of you. I know I am."

Then she gave me a small smile, with her eyes glistening with unshed tears. "Thank you. For being here. And for reminding me of the good things." Then the children began to open up as well and the boy, Timothy, often asked me about the war, with his curiosity endless. And I tried to shield him from the horrors, focusing instead on the camaraderie and resilience of the soldiers. And his younger sister, Lily, was quieter, but she loved to sit with me as I told stories— some real, some embellished—about Paul's bravery and kindness.

Then as the days turned into weeks, I found a sense of purpose that I hadn't felt in a long time. And I wasn't just passing through this time because I was making a difference, and even if it was a small one. But the pull was inevitable. And it came one morning as I was playing catch with Timothy in the backyard. And the ball slipped from my fingers, and the familiar sensation washed over me. Timothy frowned. "You okay, Michael?" Then I forced a smile. "Yeah, buddy. Just a little tired." Then when Rose came outside to call us in for lunch, I lingered for a moment, taking in the scene—the laughter, the warmth, and the life they were rebuilding despite their loss. "Thank you," I said quietly, though I knew they wouldn't hear me once I was gone.

(The Fall of Jerusalem)

Then the world spun violently as the pull overtook me again, and the now-familiar sensation of being torn from one reality and flung into another then when the spinning stopped, I landed hard on a dusty street, with my hands scraping against rough stone as I tried to steady myself. And the air was thick with the acrid scent of smoke, as it mingled with the coppery tang of blood and the cries of anguish. Then I looked around, disoriented and the city was vast, with its towering walls surrounding tightly packed buildings. And the sky was choked with dark clouds of smoke, and the distant roar of battle sent tremors through the ground. Then the sheer chaos of the scene hit me like a tidal wave. And I didn't need anyone to tell me where—or more specifically, when—I was.

Because this was Jerusalem. 70 A.D and I had read about the fall of Jerusalem in history classes and the siege by the Romans, with the destruction of the Temple, and the desperate attempts of the Jewish defenders to hold onto their city—and it was a tale of heartbreak and devastation. But seeing it firsthand was something else entirely.

Because the streets were filled with people—some fleeing, some fighting, and others frozen in fear. As the Roman soldiers clad in gleaming armor stormed through the city, and their swords slick with blood as they cut down anyone in their path. And the defenders, ragged and desperate, fought back with a ferocity born of hopelessness, while wielding makeshift weapons against the disciplined ranks of the Roman legion.

Then I ducked into an alley to avoid being caught in the chaos. And my heart was pounding, and my breath came in shallow gasps as I tried to make sense of the situation because this wasn't just a battle—it was a slaughter.

And the cries of children pierced through the cacophony, drawing my attention to a family huddled in the shadows of a crumbling building. And a woman clutched her two young sons tightly, with her eyes darting around in terror.

"Please," she whispered, her voice trembling as she spotted me. "Help us." Then I hesitated for a moment, with my mind racing becaus what could I possibly do against an army? But leaving them there felt wrong—unbearably wrong.

"Follow me," I then said, with my voice firmer than I felt.

Then they hesitated for a moment before nodding as I led them through the twisting alleys, keeping to the shadows as much as possible. Then the woman clutched her children's hands tightly, with her fear palpable. Then we managed to avoid the soldiers for a while, but as we turned a corner, a group of Romans spotted us. "Run!" I shouted, shoving the woman forward. Then she hesitated, with her eyes wide with panic, but then she took off, dragging her children with her. Then the soldiers came after me instead, with their heavy boots pounding against the cobblestones.

So I sprinted through the streets, dodging debris and leaping over fallen bodies as my lungs burned, and my muscles screamed in protest, but I didn't dare slow down. Then eventually, I managed to lose them, by ducking into an abandoned building and collapsing against the wall and my chest heaved as I tried to catch my breath, with my mind racing. And this was unlike anything I'd experienced before because the sheer brutality of it, and the utter helplessness of the people—it was overwhelming. Then over the next few weeks, I witnessed the city's descent into chaos. As food supplies dwindled, and desperation drove people to do unspeakable things. Then the defenders grew more desperate, and their numbers dwindling as the Romans closed in.

But I did what I could do to help and I joined a group of rebels who were smuggling food and supplies to those trapped in the city then as we moved through the shadows, we were always one step ahead of the Romans, but it was a losing battle and every day, the city grew quieter, and its spirit crushed under the weight of the siege. Then one day, I found myself standing near the Temple and it was a magnificent structure, and its gleaming stone walls was a testament to the faith and determination of the people who had built it. But now, it was under siege. And the Romans had breached the outer defenses, and flames licked at the base of the Temple, as black smoke billowing into the sky and I could hear the anguished cries of the priests and worshippers inside, their prayers mingling with the screams of the dying.

Then I wanted to help, but I was powerless. And all I could do was watch as the Temple burned, and its destruction was a symbol of the city's downfall. Then as the weeks dragged on, the city fell into ruin. And the streets were filled with rubble and bodies, and the once-bustling markets and homes were reduced to ashes. And the people who survived were broken, and their hope was extinguished. Then one evening, as I sat on the steps of a crumbling building, I thought about Paul, about Rose and her children because they had faced loss too, but they had found a way to keep going, and to rebuild their lives.

But here in Jerusalem, there was no rebuilding. And the city was dying, and its people were being erased from history COMPLETELY. But then the pull came again suddenly, and it was wrenching me away from the devastation. Then as the world around me dissolved, I whispered a silent prayer for the people of Jerusalem, and for their courage and resilience in the face of a unimaginable loss. Then my body felt like it was being torn apart, and dragged through time and space with an urgency that left me breathless. Then when the motion stopped, I collapsed onto soft, and damp earth. And the air was hot and heavy, and filled with the hum of insects and the distant calls of exotic animals.

Then I opened my eyes to find myself surrounded by towering trees, with their canopies forming a thick, green roof that barely let the sunlight through. And the jungle of what looked like Africa was alive, and teeming with a vibrancy that was almost overwhelming. Then for a moment, I was disoriented because this wasn't Jerusalem. And as I pushed myself up, I heard the faint rustling of movement nearby then I tensed, instinctively reaching for a weapon I didn't have. Then a group of people emerged from the dense foliage, and their clothes torn and dirty, with their faces etched with fear and exhaustion.

And then I noticed that they were survivors—men, women, and children who bore the same haunted look that I'd seen in Jerusalem. Then their eyes widened when they saw me, but they didn't run. Instead, they hesitated, and their expressions were a mix of suspicion and hope. Then one of the men stepped forward and he was tall and lean, with his dark skin glistening with sweat. And his eyes were sharp, as he scanned me with the precision of someone who had been on the run for too long.

"Who are you?" he asked, with his voice wary. "I... I don't know how I got here," I admitted. "But I was in Jerusalem and I saw what happened." Then the man's gaze softened slightly. "You fled too?" then I nodded, realizing that this must have been their story. And after the destruction of Jerusalem, some had escaped the Romans, by fleeing into the wilderness of Africa in a desperate bid for survival and it seemed that the pull had brought me here to join them. Then over the next few days, I traveled with the group as they moved deeper into the jungle. And they were cautious, and always on edge, as their fear of being discovered by Roman patrols palpable and it became clear that they had no real plan—only the instinct to run, to survive.

But the jungle was both a refuge and also a challenge. And the dense foliage offered protection, but it also made travel slow and arduous. And the heat was oppressive, as the humidity clung to us like a second skin. And food was scarce, and water had to be carefully rationed. But despite the hardships, there were moments of unexpected beauty. And the jungle was alive in a way that was almost magical. Because the brightly colored birds flitted through the trees, and their calls echoing through the canopy. While streams of crystal-clear water cut through the undergrowth, while offering brief moments of relief from the heat.

But the shadow of the Romans loomed over us, as a constant reminder of the danger we were in. Then one evening, as we huddled around a small, smokeless fire, the group's leader—a woman named Miriam—shared her story. "We were priests and merchants, mothers and fathers, and even doctors" she said, with her voice steady despite the pain in her eyes. "Then when the walls fell, we thought it was the end. But we couldn't stay. We couldn't let them take everything." Then she paused, while glancing at the children who sat close to her, and their faces streaked with dirt and weariness. "So we ran and we ran until there was nothing left but the jungle". And now we keep running, because stopping means death."

Then her words hung in the air, as a stark reminder of the stakes. And these people who had lost everything—their homes, their families, and their city, but yet they kept going, and they were driven by a fierce will to survive. Then as the weeks passed, I found myself becoming part of the group and I helped scout for food, carried the younger children when they grew too tired to walk, and stood watch at night to protect against the dangers of the jungle.

Then one day, as we rested near a river, I caught sight of Miriam sitting alone, staring at the water. And I approached her cautiously, sensing the weight of her thoughts. "You've done an incredible job keeping everyone together," I said, sitting down beside her. Then she shook her head, and her expression weary. "I've done what I had to do. But every day, it feels like we're one step closer to the end." "But we're still here," I reminded her. "So that means something." Then she turned to me, with her eyes searching mine. "So why are you here, Michael? You're not like us so she thought." Then the question caught me off guard because how could I explain the truth? That I was a traveler out of time, and flung from one era to the next without rhyme or reason? Then I replied "I don't know," I admitted. "But I want to help. And whatever happens, I'll be here."

Then her gaze softened, and she nodded. "Thank you." The turning point came one night when we heard the distant sounds of Roman voices and they were close—too close. And panic rippled through the group as we gathered what little we had and prepared to move. But it was too late. And the Romans had found us. And the clash was brutal but the survivors fought with the desperation of cornered animals, using whatever they could find as weapons. And I fought alongside them, as my heart pounded as I swung a heavy branch at the advancing soldiers.

Then we managed to hold them off long enough to escape deeper into the jungle, but the cost was high. And several of the group didn't make it, and their bodies were left behind as we fled. And in the aftermath, the survivors were quieter, with their grief heavy in the humid air. And Miriam stood apart from the group, with her shoulders slumped as she stared into the distance. "We can't keep running forever," she said softly when I approached her. Then I placed a hand on her shoulder, and my own heart heavy with the knowledge that she was right. But what choice did we have? Then as the jungle seemed to close in around us, I felt the pull again and it was sudden, like a hook dragging me backward and I didn't want to go. Not yet because these people needed me. But I was powerless against the force, and as the world dissolved around me, I whispered a silent prayer for their survival.

(The Dinosaur Age)

Then as I was dragging through the void like a violent river current. I had no control over it, no say in where or when it would take me. Then when I landed, it wasn't the humid jungle of 71 A.D anymore or the smoke-filled ruins of Jerusalem—but it was something entirely different. And the air was warm and thick, and almost tangibly alive. Then I opened my eyes and immediately realized that I wasn't in any era I could recognized. Because the towering ferns and enormous trees stretched as far as the eye could see. And the ground was soft and damp beneath me, and I littered with strange plants that looked like they'd been plucked straight out of a nature documentary about prehistory.

And then I heard it—the low, bone-rattling rumble that vibrated through the earth. And I froze, but my pulse quickening as the sound grew louder, closer. Then when the beast stepped into view, my jaw dropped. Because it was massive, and it was a creature out of nightmares and science books—with a towering, long-neck and it was a dinosaur that I recognized as a *Brachiosaurus* and its neck swayed gently as it moved through the foliage, with its enormous body shaking the ground with every step. Then for a moment, I was too stunned to move. Because I'd read about dinosaurs in school, and seen them in movies, but nothing could have prepared me for the sheer magnitude of the real thing. And this wasn't just history; this was prehistory.

And I was in the age of the dinosaurs. Then as the initial shock wore off, I began to take in my surroundings. And the world around me was lush and vibrant, and it was teeming with life. As strange bird-like creatures with long tails darted through the trees, with their calls filling the air and insects buzzed and clicked, and some of them disturbingly large. Then I stayed hidden for hours, watching the prehistoric world unfold around me. And the *Brachiosaurus* wasn't alone—because other herbivores moved in small groups, and grazed on the abundant plant life. Then I spotted a herd of *Triceratops* in the distance, and their frilled heads bobbing as they moved through the underbrush.

But it wasn't all peaceful and the shrill cries of a pack of smaller dinosaurs—*Velociraptors*, maybe—echoed through the forest as I watched them stalk their prey with a unnerving precision, and their sharp claws glinting in the dappled sunlight. Then it became clear quickly that I needed to be careful. And this wasn't just an adventure because it was also survival. Then over the next few days, I scavenged what I could to survive. And the jungle provided plenty of fruit and water, and though I was cautious about what I ate. I fashioned a makeshift spear from a sturdy branch and sharp stone, and though I doubted it would do much against some of the larger predators.

Then I found a cave to shelter in at night, and it was high enough up a rocky hill that I felt relatively safe. But still, sleep didn't come easily. And every sound—was a distant roar of a carnivore, and the rustling of leaves—set my nerves on edge. Then one evening, as the sun set in a spectacular blaze of orange and red, I spotted a massive creature stalking the plains below. And its head was enormous, with its teeth gleaming even in the fading light.

A *Tyrannosaurus rex.* And it was every bit as terrifying as I'd imagined. And the sheer power and presence of the beast were overwhelming. But I watched it tear into a carcass, and its jaws working with brutal efficiency. And the sound of bones snapping echoed up the hill, sending chills down my spine. Then from that moment on, I was even more careful. Then the knowledge that such predators roamed this world made every step a calculated risk.

Then one afternoon, as I was exploring the edge of a river, I heard a sound that didn't belong—a human voice. "Help! Over here!" Then my heart leaped because I wasn't alone. Then I followed the voice to find a man clinging to a fallen tree in the middle of the river and the current was strong, while threatening to pull him under. Without thinking, and I waded into the water, and the force of it almost knocking me off my feet. "Hold on!" I shouted, grabbing the tree and helping him climb onto it. Then together, we managed to drag it to the shore. And then I noticed that he was older, maybe in his late 50s, with a grizzled beard and weathered skin. And his clothes were tattered, and his eyes were wide with disbelief. "Who... who are you?" he stammered. "Michael," I said, still catching my breath. "Who are you?" "Dr. Alan Strauss," he said, shaking his head as if to clear it. "I... I think I'm dreaming." I laughed bitterly. "You're not. Trust me." Then it turned out Dr. Strauss had been part of some sort of experiment involving time manipulation. And something had gone wrong, and he'd ended up here—just like me.

But having someone else to talk to was a relief, and though Strauss was skeptical of my story at first. Together, we worked to survive, pooling our knowledge and resources. Then as the days turned into weeks, I began to notice something strange and the animals were acting differently—restless, and almost frantic and even the massive herbivores seemed uneasy, with their movements hurried as if they sensed something coming. And then I saw it one night, as I stood outside the cave, and a streak of light appeared in the sky. And it was small at first, and almost beautiful, but it grew larger with each passing moment, and its fiery tail stretching across the heavens.

And I knew what it was. "Alan," I whispered, with my voice trembling. "It's the asteroid." And the one that would end the dinosaurs. And we had no time to prepare but the impact was catastrophic, shaking the earth with a force I could barely comprehend. And the air filled with ash and debris, as it blotted out the sun and plunging the world into darkness. But Strauss and I huddled in the cave, with the ground trembling beneath us as the world outside fell apart. Then the roars of terrified animals filled the air, and their fear echoing my own. And I didn't know if we would survive. Plus I didn't know if the pull would come again to save me or if this was where my journey would end but I held onto hope because it was all I had left. Then the pull came again, just as the cave crumbled around me. And I had no time to think or prepare, and no chance to grab onto anything solid before I was swept away and it was always like this—chaotic, unpredictable—but this time it felt different. And it wasn't just the usual dizziness or weightlessness but it felt deeper, heavier, as if I were being dragged through layers of time instead of moments.

(Noah & The Flood)

And this time the pull felt heavier and it wasn't just disorienting—it was suffocating. Then when I landed the air itself felt different, it was thick with humidity and heavy with an almost electric charge. Then I opened my eyes to see a landscape that seemed on the brink of something catastrophic. And rolling hills stretched into the distance, but the sky above was a swirling canvas of gray clouds, dark and ominous. And the air carried a faint scent of rain, but it hadn't fallen yet and there was a tension, a sense of waiting, as though the entire world was holding its breath.

Then that's when I saw him and he was a figure that stood atop of a hill, and his silhouette framed against the turbulent sky. And he was older, with his long beard streaked with gray and his face deeply lined, but his posture was strong, purposeful. And he was surrounded by what appeared to be stacks of wood and tools. So I approached cautiously, and my footsteps crunched against the dry earth. Then he turned at the sound, and his piercing eyes met mine.

"Who are you?" he asked, his voice low but steady. Then I hesitated because what could I possibly say that wouldn't sound insane? "I... I'm a traveler," I replied finally. "I've come from far away." Then he studied me for a long moment, then nodded, as though my vague answer was sufficient. "You've arrived at a pivotal time, traveler. There is much work to be done." And it didn't take long for me to piece together where—and when—I was because this man was Noah, with those stacks of wood? were the beginnings of the Ark. Then he spoke with a urgency, describing a divine command that he had received: and a flood was coming, and one that would cleanse the Earth of its wickedness. Then he had been tasked with building a massive vessel to save his family and two of every kind of animal. And it sounded impossible, but the conviction in his voice left no room for doubt. And I didn't know if my presence here was accidental or part of some greater plan, but I couldn't ignore the gravity of the situation so if I could help, I had to.

Then for weeks, I worked alongside Noah and his sons and the tasks were monumental. And the Ark was enormous, and its frame rising higher with each passing day. And the smell of sawdust and pitch clung to my skin, and my muscles ached from the relentless labor. And Noah was tireless, with his determination unwavering. As he worked from dawn until the last light of day, with his faith driving him forward. And his sons followed his lead, with their movements precise and coordinated and I couldn't help but admire their dedication.

Then as the Ark neared completion, something incredible began to happen. And animals began to arrive.

And it first started with a pair of deer emerging from the forest, with their movements calm and deliberate. Then came the birds, with their wings casting fleeting shadows as they landed near the Ark. Then soon, the plains were filled with creatures of every kind—lions, elephants, bears, and countless others. And it was surreal, watching them march in pairs, as though they understood their purpose. Then Noah's sons guided the animals onto the Ark, with their voices calm and steady. And the sheer logistics of the task were overwhelming, but everything seemed to fall into place.

Then one evening, as we rested by the fire, I asked Noah how he could remain so steadfast in the face of such an enormous challenge. "My faith sustains me," he replied simply. "and the Creator has a plan, and I am but a servant fulfilling my role." Then I envied his certainty because my own journey had been a chaotic whirlwind, and each new destination throwing me into the unknown. But Noah? He was grounded, and his path clear. And as the days passed, the sky grew darker, and the clouds thicker. And a sense of foreboding hung over us, an unspoken acknowledgment that the flood was imminent.

Then villagers from nearby settlements began to gather, with their faces a mix of curiosity and ridicule. And they mocked Noah, by calling him mad, and their laughter echoing across the hills. But Noah paid them no mind. And he continued his work, with his focus unshaken. Then one night, as I sat beside him, I asked if their words ever got to him. "They do not understand," he said quietly. "But they will, when it is too late." And his words sent a chill down my spine. Then the rain began as a soft patter, and almost gentle. But it didn't take long for it to intensify. And by the second day, it was relentless, and the sky unleashing torrents of water that soaked the earth and filled the rivers. Then the villagers' laughter turned to panic. As they flocked to higher ground, and their cries of fear cutting through the storm. Then by the seventh day, the floodwaters were rising rapidly. And the Ark was complete, and its massive frame towering above the landscape. And Noah's family and the animals were safely aboard, but I hesitated at the entrance.

Because this was their story, and not mine and I didn't belong there. Then Noah appeared beside me, with his gaze steady. "You've done your part, traveler now, trust in the Creator." Then before I could respond, the pull came again. And the world blurred and shifted, and the roar of the flood fading into silence. Then as I was swept away, I couldn't help but wonder if I would ever return to a time where I truly belonged—or if my journey was far from over. Then when I landed, the air was clear, and the sky was a soft gradient of blues and whites. And I was in a valley lush with greenery, and a stark contrast to the chaotic scenes of the flood I had left behind.

Then I stood atop a small hill, overlooking what appeared to be a settlement. Then a wooden structure, modest but sturdy, stood at its center. And fields stretched outward, and dotted with grazing animals and bustling figures. Then my heart raced as I recognized one of them: Noah. And though his posture remained upright, his movements were deliberate. And his beard, was now entirely white, and flowed like a river down his chest. But yet there was a lightness to him, a sense of peace and I hadn't seen before.

Then I approached him cautiously, and unsure how he would react to seeing me again. Then when he finally noticed me, his eyes widened in recognition. "Traveler," he said, his voice as steady as I remembered. "You've returned." Then I nodded, unable to suppress a smile. "I had to see how you were doing. How the world was rebuilding." Then he gestured for me to follow him, leading me to the wooden structure at the center of the settlement. And inside, it was warm and inviting, and the air filled with the smell of freshly baked bread. And his family was there—his sons, their wives, and grandchildren who had been born since the flood. Then Noah introduced me as an "old friend," and they welcomed me with a kindness that was almost overwhelming.

Then over the weeks that followed, I immersed myself in their lives. And the land around them was fertile, bursting with life in a way that felt almost miraculous. And crops grew tall, while the animals thrived. And it was as if the earth itself was eager to start anew. Then Noah spent his days overseeing the settlement, ensuring that everything ran smoothly. Then he spoke often of the Creator's covenant, and the promise symbolized by the rainbow that occasionally arched across the sky. "The flood was a reset," he explained then one evening as we sat by a fire. "A chance for humanity to begin again. But it is up to us to honor that chance, to live righteously and care for this earth." And his words resonated with me. Even though I was merely a traveler in his time, I couldn't help but think about my own world. And were we honoring our own chance, or were we hurtling toward our own version of the flood?

Then one afternoon, I found myself walking along the banks of a river that cut through the valley and the water was calm, with its surface reflecting the vibrant greens of the surrounding trees. And it was a far cry from the torrential waters that I had witnessed during the flood. Then Noah joined me, and his hands clasped behind his back. "This place is beautiful," I said, breaking the silence. "It is," he agreed. "But beauty is fragile and it must be nurtured, and protected." Then I hesitated before asking the question that had been on my mind since I arrived. "Do you ever wonder why you were chosen? Or why your family was spared?" Then he stopped walking, with his gaze fixed on the horizon. "I have asked myself that question many times but The Creator saw something in us—faith, perhaps, or resilience. But it is not for me to question. It is for me to act." Then his humility struck me because despite all he had endured, he bore no resentment, and no arrogance and he simply accepted his role and carried on.

Then as the weeks passed, I grew closer to Noah and his family. And his sons shared stories of their journey aboard the Ark, and their voices tinged with both awe and sorrow. And they spoke of the loss they had witnessed, and the weight of being the sole survivors of a world washed away. But they also spoke of hope, of their determination to build a better future. And the children were a source of joy, with their laughter echoing through the valley. And they were the embodiment of that hope, as unburdened by the past and full of potential. Then one evening, as the sun dipped below the horizon, painting the sky in shades of orange and pink, Noah's youngest grandson approached me.

"Are you staying with us forever?" he asked, his wide eyes filled with innocence. Then I knelt to meet his gaze. "I don't know," I admitted. "But I'm glad I'm here now." And though I didn't want to admit it, I could feel the pull beginning to stir within me again. And my time here was coming to an end, and though I didn't know where—or when—I would end up next I confided in Noah one last time, sharing my fears and uncertainties about my journey. "Your path is unlike any I've known," he said thoughtfully. "But perhaps that is the Creator's design because you are a witness, and a bridge between times so do not fear the unknown, traveler and embrace it." Then his words stayed with me as I stood at the edge of the settlement, while watching the people I had come to care for go about their lives.

(The Stone Age)

Then the pull came again with full force and when I landed the air was dense and carried a unmistakable scent of earth—raw, untamed, and ancient. Then I blinked against and realized that the dim light was the light of of the Stone Age's sun, which seemed muted by a haze that hung perpetually in the sky. Then when I looked around, I was surrounded by a landscape so primal it felt almost otherworldly because towering mountains loomed in the distance, and their peaks capped with snow, and while sprawling forests covered the land like a thick green carpet in every direction, I could hear the calls of wild animals, some familiar and others entirely foreign.

Then as I wandered, I saw no signs of a civilization because I had grown used to seeing them in my time jumps, but instead, the world was quiet, and save for the rustling of leaves and the occasional birdcall. And the air was heavy with possibility—and a world untouched by industry, unspoiled by time. And it wasn't long before I stumbled upon a group of humans. And they were unlike any I had ever seen, with their faces roughened by exposure to the elements, and their bodies clad in animal skins. And they moved with a cautious grace, with their every action deliberate and purposeful.

And they saw me before I could decide whether to approach. And a man with a stone-tipped spear barked a sharp sound, and the group turned to face me. Then for a moment, I thought they might attack, but then a older woman stepped forward, with her eyes narrowing as she studied me. Then I raised my hands in what I hoped was a universal gesture of peace. Then slowly, she lowered the stick she carried and gestured for me to follow them. Then I noticed that the tribe lived in a clearing by a river, and their homes little more than shelters made of branches and animal hides. And smoke rose from a fire at the center of their camp, where several people were cooking meat over the flames and the scent made my stomach rumble.

Then as I was led into their midst, I could feel their eyes on me—curious, wary, and maybe even a little fearful. Then the woman who had first approached me seemed to be their leader, and she spoke to them in a language I couldn't understand. Then over the days that followed, I began to observe and learn. And communication was difficult, but the tribe's actions spoke louder than words. As they hunted, gathered, and prepared food with an efficiency that left me in awe. And they crafted tools from stone and bone, with their hands moving with a practiced skill.

Then I watched as they painted intricate designs on the walls of a nearby cave, with their fingers smearing ochre and charcoal to create images of animals and hunts. And these paintings weren't just art—and they were stories, records of their lives and beliefs. And what struck me most was their sense of community. And every task was shared, and every success celebrated together. And the children played near the fire, with their laughter ringing out like music, while the elders told stories in hushed tones.

Then I realized that this was the foundation of society, the very beginning of human cooperation and culture. And they had no written language, no formal laws, but they had each other, and that was enough. Then one evening, the tribe gathered around the fire to feast on a successful hunt and I had helped track a large deer earlier that day, and though I hadn't done much to contribute, they handed me a piece of meat as if I were one of them.

Then the firelight danced on their faces as they sang and clapped, with their voices rising and falling in a rhythm that seemed to echo the heartbeat of the earth itself.

Then as time passed I noticed that Life in the Stone Age wasn't without its challenges and I witnessed their struggle to fend off predators—and massive wolves with yellow eyes that prowled the edges of their camp. And I saw them mourn the loss of a young hunter who had fallen while trying to scale a rocky cliff. But despite the hardships, they endured. They adapted and it was a resilience born from necessity, and a determination to survive in a world that offered no guarantees. Then I found myself marveling at their ingenuity. And they knew which plants could be eaten and which were poisonous. And they used fire not just for warmth but for crafting tools and hardening the tips of their spears. Then over time, I became more than just an observer. And the tribe began to accept me, and I started to contribute in small ways and I helped them gather firewood, carried water from the river, and even attempted to learn their language. Then one of the children, a boy no older than five, took a particular liking to me. And he would follow me around, mimicking my movements and laughing at my attempts to speak their words. And his name, I learned, was something like "Rahk," and his curiosity reminded me of the children I had met in other times.

Then one night, as I sat by the fire, the leader of the tribe approached me. And she placed her hand on my shoulder and said something I couldn't fully understand, but her tone was warm, and almost maternal so I nodded, and for the first time since arriving in this era, I felt a sense of belonging and yet, even as I grew closer to the tribe, I could feel the familiar pull building within me. And my time here was running out, and though I didn't know where I would go next, the thought of leaving filled me with a deep sadness. Then before the pull could take me, I decided to leave something behind. Using a piece of charcoal from the fire, Then I added my own mark to the wall of the cave—as a simple drawing of a traveler, standing beneath the stars. Then as the pull finally came, I stood at the edge of the camp, watching the tribe as they went about their evening routines. And I hoped that, in some small way, my presence had made a difference. And then I was gone, and the Stone Age started to fade into the ether as I hurtled toward my next destination.

Then I blinked, as I was disoriented, and the rush of swirling light and sensations spat me out onto solid ground. And the air was crisp, and it carried the faint smell of pine and damp earth. And for the first time in what felt like ages, I recognized the world around me—and it was not the ancient past or some distant future, but it was a time close to my time and it was unmistakably my own time period then I saw a craving that read "Joe was here 2008" and then that confirmed that I was close to my time. And the hum of distant highways and the faint buzz of airplanes overhead whispered modernity. Then I collapsed onto the soft ground, and the familiar scent of the grass that was beneath me feeling like a warm embrace.

Then the sun hovered low in the sky, casting a long, golden shadow through the trees. And I wasn't sure exactly where I was, but something about this place felt familiar. So as I raised to my feet, I took in my surroundings—and a dense forest with a rocky outcrop looming nearby. Then I saw it: the mouth of a cave etched into the hillside. Then a jolt of recognition coursed through me, and like a long-buried memory clawing its way to the surface it couldn't be... could it? I thought Then my heart raced as I stumbled toward the cave, and my legs moved faster than my mind could process. And the entrance was as I remembered it—as it was jagged and uninviting, yet irresistibly intriguing. Then the sunlight barely reached inside, casting only the faintest glow on the rough stone walls.

So I stepped inside, and my breath caught in my throat because there it was, right where I had left it. My mark. And the figure I had drawn with trembling hands so long ago—or rather, so many millennia's ago. And The image was faint, and its charcoal lines faded by time and the elements, but it was still there. And a simple drawing of a traveler beneath the stars. My traveler. Me. Then I reached out, my fingers hovering just above the surface of the stone, as if touching it would somehow shatter the fragile connection between past and present. But I couldn't help myself then my fingers brushed against the wall, feeling the slight indentations where the charcoal had once bitten into the rock. And a strange mixture of emotions washed over me—pride, disbelief, and an overwhelming sense of wonder. This was proof, undeniable proof, that everything I had experienced was real and maybe time brought me right here just as a reminder that every time that I was entering was real.

Then as I traced the lines of the drawing, memories flooded back. And I remembered the tribe, and their faces etched with both hardship and joy. Then I remembered the boy, Rahk, laughing as he mimicked my movements. And I remembered the leader's firm but gentle presence and the way they had made me feel like one of their own. And I could still hear the crackle of their fire, and the smell of the roasted meat, and feel the rough texture of their tools in my hands. And it was as if the Stone Age was reaching out to me across the chasm of time, pulling me back into its embrace.

Then for weeks, I returned to the cave every day, studying the drawings on its walls because my mark wasn't the only one, of course. And the tribe's images of hunts, animals, and abstract patterns were all there, vivid and alive in their own way. So I began to see connections that I hadn't noticed before—and symbols and shapes that seemed to tell stories of their lives, their fears, and their hopes. Then it was like deciphering an ancient language and one that spoke not in words but in the raw, unfiltered essence of humanity. Then being here, seeing my mark preserved through time, gave me a sense of purpose that I hadn't felt in a long while. And it was a reminder that no matter how far I traveled, and no matter how lost I felt, that I had left an imprint—both literal and metaphorical. But it also raised questions. And had the tribe seen my drawing after I left? What had they thought of it? And had they wondered about the strange traveler who had appeared in their midst and then vanished without a trace? Then one day, as I sat in the cave, a thought struck me. What if my mark had inspired them in some way? What if, in their own time, they had looked at it and felt the same awe and wonder that I felt now?

Then as the days turned into weeks, I found myself returning to the cave not just to study the drawings but to reflect. And I thought about the people I had met during my journeys—Noah, Paul, the soldiers, and the workers of the Industrial Revolution. And each of them had shaped me in some way, and I could only hope I had done the same for them. Then the cave became my sanctuary, a place where time seemed to stand still. And while sitting there, surrounded by the echoes of the past, I felt a strange sense of peace. And for the first time in what felt like forever, I wasn't running or fighting or struggling to survive. And I was simply... being.

Then of course, it couldn't last and one evening, as the sun dipped below the horizon and the cave filled with shadows, I felt it—the familiar pull in my chest, that strange, irresistible force that had dragged me through time again and again. And I knew what it meant and that my time here was over and I was not done with my journey through time yet. So as the pull grew stronger, I stood and took one last look at the drawing on the wall. And it seemed to glow faintly in the dim light, as if bidding me farewell. Then I pressed my hand against the cool stone and whispered, "Thank you." And then the world dissolved into light, the cave vanishing as I hurtled toward whatever awaited me next.

(Sodom & Gomorrah)

Then as the transition begun it was violent and this time, it was more than any I had experienced before. And I felt like I was being torn apart, then pulled through a narrow tunnel of blinding light and deafening silence. Then when I emerged on the other side, I found myself gasping for air, sprawled on dusty ground beneath a searing sun. Then as I slowly sat up, the landscape came into focus. And the heat was oppressive, while radiating off the arid earth in shimmering waves. And around me stretched a barren wilderness, punctuated by occasional clusters of olive trees and low shrubs. And in the distance, I could see two cities nestled in a fertile plain, then their structures gleaming in the sunlight.

Then a sinking feeling gripped me and I didn't need to know where—or rather, when—I was to feel the weight of the moment. But as I stood and dusted myself off, a name floated to the forefront of my mind: Sodom. Then the realization hit me like a punch to the gut because it was Sodom and Gomorrah, the cities infamous for their corruption and ultimate destruction and I had read the biblical account, but now I was standing on the cusp of one of history's—or myth's—most catastrophic events.

Then I began walking towards the cities, unsure of what else to do. And my instincts told me to tread carefully because this wasn't just any time period; this was a moment of fraught with divine intervention and mortal peril. Then as I crested a hill, I spotted a group of people traveling along a dusty road below and they were heavily laden with supplies and livestock, and their movements hurried and anxious. And among them was a man who exuded a quiet authority, with his weathered face lined with both wisdom and weariness and I didn't have to guess who he was and the was Abraham. So after taking a deep breath, I descended down the hill and I approached the group. Then as I got closer, several men stepped forward, and their hands resting on the hilts of their weapons.

"I mean no harm," I said quickly, raising my hands in a gesture of peace. Then Abraham stepped forward, studying me with piercing eyes. "Who are you, stranger, and what brings you to this land?" And his voice was calm but carried an edge of suspicion. "My name is Michael," I replied, choosing my words carefully. "And I've... traveled far to be here and I believe I can help." Then Abraham's expression didn't soften, but he nodded after a moment. "Ok and we are on our way to rescue my nephew Lot and his family because they are in Sodom, a place doomed to destruction and if you wish to help, you must be prepared for great danger." Then I nodded, feeling the weight of his words. "I'm ready. "I finally replied

Then we began our journey and the journey to Sodom was tense and fraught with unease. And as we approached the city gates, the air seemed to grow heavier and it charged with an almost tangible sense of foreboding. And the city itself was a sprawling maze of narrow streets and tall, weathered buildings. And then the noise of shouting merchants and laughing revelers echoed around us while masking the underlying tension that seemed to permeate the air. Then Abraham's plan was simple: find Lot, and his wife, and their daughters and get them out before it was too late but that was easier said than done in a city teeming with vice and suspicion.

So then we moved quickly through the streets, while keeping our heads low and our eyes were sharp. And the city's inhabitants were a motley mix of traders, laborers, and those who lived off the misfortune of others. And their gazes lingered on us for too long, then their expressions ranged from curious to hostile. Then finally, we reached Lot's home—a modest but sturdy structure near the edge of the city. And Abraham knocked on the door, with his urgency clear. Then when Lot opened it, his relief was palpable. "Uncle!" he exclaimed, pulling Abraham into a quick embrace. "What are you doing here?" "There's no time to explain," Abraham said. "You must gather your family and leave the city at once because it will soon be destroyed." Then Lot hesitated, his expression torn between disbelief and fear. "Destroyed? By whom?" "By God," Abraham said simply.

Then after convincing Lot to leave was only half of the battle. And his wife and daughters were reluctant, with their lives too entwined with the city to abandon it easily. But as the hours passed and the air grew heavier with an almost supernatural tension, they finally agreed. Then we left under the cover of darkness, while slipping through the city's winding streets as quietly as possible. And I could feel the eyes of the city on us, and shadows flitting in and out of view as if the very walls were alive. Then at one point, a group of men confronted us, with their intentions far from friendly. And my heart pounded as Abraham stepped forward, and with his voice firm but calm as he persuaded them to let us pass and I don't know how he did it—or whether it was sheer will power or divine intervention—but they relented, and we continued on our way.

Then as we neared the outskirts of the city, a sudden, blinding light lit up the sky. And the ground trembled beneath our feet, and a deafening roar filled the air. "Run!" Abraham shouted, with his voice barely audible over the chaos. So we broke into a sprint, and the heat of the oncoming destruction licking at our backs. And I risked a glance over my shoulder and immediately wished I hadn't because the city was engulfed in flames, and its buildings crumbling as fire and brimstone rained down from the heavens. Then Lot's wife faltered, and her steps slowed as she turned to look back. "No!" I shouted, reaching out to stop her. But it was too late. And she froze in place, with her body stiffening as if turned to stone.

And we didn't have time to mourn because the destruction was relentless, and the ground cracked splitting beneath us as we fled toward the safety of the hills. Then when we finally reached the safety of a cave in the mountains, we collapsed in exhaustion. Then Lot and his daughters wept for their losses, and their grief was raw and unrestrained. And Abraham stood at the cave's entrance, with his face a mask of sorrow and resolve. Then I sat in silence, trying to process everything I had just witnessed because the destruction of Sodom and Gomorrah wasn't just a story anymore; it was a searing reality burned into my memory. But amidst the devastation, I felt a glimmer of hope. And Lot and his family had survived, a testament to the resilience of the human spirit and the power of faith. Then as I looked out over the smoldering ruins of the cities below, I couldn't help but wonder what would come next. For them, for me, and for the countless lives that would follow in the wake of this ancient tragedy. Then the familiar pull of teleportation was more jarring this time. And my limbs felt heavy, and my mind hazy, as though I was dragging by the weight of my journey behind me. Then when the light faded and my vision returned, I was standing under a sky brushed with the deep orange and purple hues of twilight. And the air smelled of the dry earth and wood smoke, tinged with the faint aroma of livestock. Then I looked around and recognized the terrain—as a wide expanse of rolling hills that dotted with tents and herds of sheep. And the memory of Sodom's destruction was still vivid in my mind, and this land bore a resemblance to the wilderness where Lot and I had fled. But something was different. Then in the distance, a cluster of figures moved about a sprawling camp. And the sound of voices, muffled by the breeze, reached my ears. And as I approached, the voices grew clearer, and among them, one stood out—calm, measured, and familiar. Then my heart skipped a beat. "Michael?" The voice was tinged with disbelief and... recognition. Then I froze, and then, emerging from one of the tents, I saw him. Abraham. But this was not the same Abraham I had journeyed with because his beard was longer, streaked with white, and his posture was stooped with age. And his eyes, though, were as sharp as ever, scanning me as though I were an apparition.

"It can't be," he murmured, taking a hesitant step toward me. "Abraham," I said. "It's me." he said as his hand trembled as he raised it to point at me. "You have not aged a day since we parted ways." "I... I don't know how to explain it," I stammered. "I've been traveling—through time, through places and I don't control it." Then Abraham's expression softened into one of awe. "Then you are no ordinary man. Perhaps God has a purpose for you beyond my understanding." Then over the following days, I stayed with Abraham and his household. And he was now settled in a region near Hebron, where he had established a sizable camp and despite his advanced age, he remained a revered figure among his people, who treated him with the utmost respect.

And Abraham was eager to hear about my travels. And I recounted my experiences, omitting the parts that might have seemed too fantastical—dinosaurs, futuristic cities, and industrial revolutions because those didn't fit into his worldview. So instead, I focused on the events surrounding Noah, and the times he might recognize. Then in return, he shared stories of his life since the destruction of Sodom. And he spoke of Sarah, who had passed away, and of Isaac, his promised son, who was now a young man. And there was pride in his voice when he spoke of Isaac, but also a trace of concern, as though the weight of divine promises but still he pressed heavily upon him.

"I never thought I would see you again," he said one evening as we sat under the stars. "because you appeared in my life like a fleeting shadow, and only to vanish just as quickly. And now, here you are, unchanged, while I... I am an old man." And I didn't know how to respond because the truth was, I hadn't expected to see him again either. But sitting there, listening to his steady voice and feeling the warmth of the fire between us, I felt a sense of peace that had eluded me for what felt like lifetimes. Then one day, Abraham asked me to accompany him on a journey. "There is something I must do," he said, and his tone was heavy with significance and he didn't elaborate, but I could tell it was important. So we packed provisions and set out early and the next morning, as we ascended a mountain that overlooked the camp. Along the way, I noticed the solemnity in Abraham's demeanor because he was a man weighed down by duty, but also by something more profound—faith.

And at the summit, he knelt to pray. And I stood a respectful distance away, while watching as he poured his heart out to a God and I could not see but whose presence I could almost feel. Then when he finished, he turned to me. "Michael, your presence here is no coincidence. You were sent to remind me of God's promises, to strengthen my resolve." And I didn't know what to say and I wasn't sure if I had been sent by divine intervention or if I was simply caught in the chaotic tides of time. But seeing Abraham's conviction, I couldn't help but feel that my presence here mattered. Then as the days turned into weeks, I found myself reflecting on Abraham's unwavering faith and despite the trials he had faced—and the loss of loved ones, the burden of divine commands—he remained steadfast.

"You have traveled through time and seen more than any man could comprehend," he said to me one evening. "But even you must realize that life is not about understanding every mystery. It is about trusting in something greater than yourself." And his words stayed with me long after our conversations ended. And Abraham's life was a testament to the power of faith, and while I didn't share his exact beliefs, I couldn't deny its strength. Then one morning, as the sun rose over the hills, I felt the now-familiar pull of teleportation. And I knew my time with Abraham was coming to an end. "I think I'm leaving again," I told him, as my voice tinged with regret. Then Abraham placed a hand on my shoulder. "Then go with God, Michael. Wherever He leads you, trust that you are part of His plan." Then as the light enveloped me and Abraham's figure faded from view, I felt a strange mixture of sadness and hope. Because I didn't know where—or when—I would end up next, but I carried Abraham's words with me. Faith. Trust. And Purpose because they were lessons I would not forget.

(The Ice Age)

Then a biting cold hit me before I even opened my eyes after I was pulled in time again. And my body shivered involuntarily, and my breath escaped in sharp puffs of steam. Then when I finally looked around, my heart sank. And the landscape was stark and alien—a desolate world locked in ice. Towering glaciers loomed in the distance, and their jagged surfaces glinting in the weak light of the sun, which hung low in a perpetually gray sky. And the air smelled sharp and metallic, and the wind howled with an unrelenting ferocity.
I was in the Ice Age.

And the far reach of modern human existence seemed like a harsh teacher. And there were no warm houses, no beds to return to. Instead, I found myself standing ankle-deep in snow, with my sneakers utterly useless against the biting chill. And every part of my body screamed for warmth, and I knew I wouldn't last long like this. "Okay, Michael," I muttered to myself, my voice swallowed by the howling wind. "Think. Survive. Adapt." Then I staggered forward, with my muscles stiff from the cold. And in the distance, I spotted a cluster of rocks that formed a natural shelter. So with no better options, I made my way toward them, my legs dragging through the snow. And the cave wasn't large, but it was enough to block out the relentless wind and inside, I found traces of soot on the walls— proof that fire had once been kindled here. And I wasn't alone in this timeline. Somewhere out there, people were surviving. If they could do it, so could I.

But It took hours of shivering and strategizing before I decided to venture out again. And my fingers were numb, but I had managed to gather enough sticks and dry grass to fashion a crude torch. And with the spark of flint stones— another lucky find near the cave I lit the torch and moved deeper into this frozen world. And it wasn't long before I encountered them: a small band of humans, wrapped in thick animal furs, with their faces weathered and cautious and their eyes widened as they saw me, a figure clad in strange, colorful clothes. Then one of them, a tall man with a spear, stepped forward and his expression was both wary and curious. "Ak-tan?" he said, his voice deep and guttural. "I... I mean no harm," I said, raising my hands in a universal gesture of peace. Then the man tilted his head, clearly not understanding my words. Then he glanced at my torch, then back at me, with his brow furrowed. Then finally, he gestured for me to follow.

Then he brought me to his camp—a cluster of tents made from animal hides, nestled against the side of a glacier. And the warmth of a central fire was a welcome relief, and the smell of roasting meat filled the air. And the clan consisted of about twenty people, ranging from elders with graying hair to children who peeked at me from behind their mothers. And it took time to earn their trust and at first, they kept their distance, murmuring among themselves in a language I couldn't understand. But I made myself useful and I showed them how to better insulate their tents using layers of snow, which acted as natural insulation plus I helped sharpen their tools with stones I found near the river. Then slowly, they began to accept me as one of their own. And the man who had first approached me—whom I came to know as Kalan—became my guide and through gestures and simple words, he taught me how to hunt, and how to recognize animal tracks, and how to avoid the more dangerous predators that roamed the Ice Age, like saber-toothed cats and mammoths.

And life in the Ice Age was brutally simple. And every day was a fight for survival. And the clan hunted, gathered, and celebrated every small victory and successful hunts, and a fire that lasted through the night, or a baby's first steps. Then one night, as we huddled around the fire, Kalan began to paint on the cave walls. And his fingers, dipped in red and black pigments, moved with practiced ease. As he drew scenes of hunts, of great beasts brought down by spears, and of the stars that guided them. Then I watched in awe. And this was history unfolding before my eyes—as the beginnings of human expression, and the roots of art and storytelling. "Ak-tan," Kalan said, pointing at a figure he had drawn. And it was unmistakably me, holding a torch, surrounded by the clan. Then I smiled, feeling a strange mix of pride and sadness. Because I was part of their story now, and even if only for a brief moment.

And the most unforgettable moment came during a hunt. While Kalan and a group of men had tracked a herd of mammoths to a frozen plain I had no choice but to join them, despite my fear. And the sight of the mammoths was breathtaking because they were massive, and with their shaggy fur and curved tusks made them look both majestic and terrifying. Then the hunters moved with precision, coordinating their attack with grunts and hand signals. Then when the first spear struck, the mammoth let out a deafening roar. Chaos erupted as the hunters closed in, their spears finding their marks. As I stood at the edge of the fray, heart pounding, until Kalan shouted at me to help. Then I grabbed a spear and threw it with all my strength. And the weapon struck the mammoth's side, and though it was a small wound, and it was enough to help bring the beast down. Then the hunters erupted in cheers, and their victory palpable. And that night, the clan celebrated with a feast. As I sat by the fire, chewing on roasted mammoth meat, and I felt a strange sense of belonging. Because for all the hardships, there was something profoundly human about this time—about their resilience, their community, and their will to survive.

Then as weeks passed, or so it seemed because I lost track of time in the endless cycle of hunting, gathering, and surviving. But one night, as I lay in my fur-lined tent a chill of the Ice Age was now a familiar companion. And I had grown accustomed to its unyielding grip on the world, and its stark beauty etched into glaciers and snowfields. But this time, when the light deposited me back into the frozen wilderness, something felt... different. And the air seemed heavier, tinged with an unnatural static. Then the sky grew darker, as if the sun itself had withdrawn from this part of time. And then I saw it—a faint, flickering glow in the distance, like fire but not quite. So out of curiosity I outweighed caution by wrapping myself tighter in the furs I had scavenged, and I trudged toward the light, with my boots crunching through the snow. Then as I got closer, I realized it wasn't a fire at all It was some kind of... portal and a swirling mass of light and energy, that pulsated with a rhythm that made the air hum.

Then standing before it was a figure—clad in sleek, metallic clothing that shimmered faintly in the dim light. And the person had their back to me, seemingly engrossed in adjusting a device strapped to their arm.
"Uh... hello?" I called out, with my voice tentative. And the figure froze, then turned sharply. Then my breath caught in my throat because the traveler wasn't like anyone I'd ever seen but they had a humanoid appearance, but their features were sharper, and more angular. And their eyes glowed faintly, as a soft blue that seemed to pierce through me. "Who are you?" I asked, instinctively stepping back. Then the traveler tilted their head, studying me. Then, to my surprise, they spoke—in perfect, unaccented English. "I could ask you the same question," they said, their tone calm but firm. "You don't belong here." "I know," I replied, raising my hands to show I meant no harm. "Believe me, I've been trying to get back to my own time, but it's... complicated."

Then the traveler's expression softened slightly and the traveler gestured for me to approach, and I did so cautiously. And up close, their clothing seemed to be made of a material I couldn't identify, something that shimmered and shifted like liquid metal. "I'm Michael," I said. "I'm from 2025. And I'm... stuck." Then the traveler nodded slowly. "I'm Aelira," she said. "And I'm from 4128. And it seems we're both in the wrong place at the wrong time." Then my jaw dropped. "4128? You're... from the future?" Then Aelira gave a small smile. "Yes the far future, from your perspective. And I'm part of a reconnaissance team studying temporal anomalies in the timeline. And judging by your presence here, I'd say we've found one." "Temporal anomalies?" I echoed. "Yes," they said, gesturing toward the swirling portal. "Because time isn't as linear as you think, Michael. It's more like a web—fragile and interconnected and something—or someone—has disrupted the flow, and now we're all being pulled into the wrong threads."

And Aelira seemed wary of me at first, but as I explained my story—my experiments with astral projection, and my accidental journey through time she began to trust me. Then she scanned me with her wrist device. And a holographic display floated in the air, and filled with symbols I couldn't decipher. "Your temporal signature is... unusual but it's no wonder you can't return home." "Can you help me?" I asked in desperation creeping into my voice. Then Aelira hesitated. "Perhaps," she said. "But first, I need to stabilize the rift here and if it collapses, we're both trapped." Then for the next several days—weeks, maybe—we worked together. And Aelira showed me how to gather materials from the Ice Age environment and how to reinforce the portal's structure. And it was surreal, watching her manipulate advanced technology amidst the primal wilderness. Then in return, I shared my knowledge of survival. And Aelira, for all her technological prowers, was unfamiliar with the harsh realities of this time. So I taught her how to build fires, how to track game, and how to navigate the icy terrain.

Then during our time together, we talked about everything—our lives, our worlds, our perspectives and on time and existence. "In my era," Aelira said one night as we huddled near the fire, "time travel is a tool for exploration and understanding but it's dangerous because one misstep, one ripple, and the consequences can be catastrophic." "And that's what I'm afraid of," I admitted. "'Because I've seen so many timelines already. And what if my presence is changing them?" Then Aelira gave me a thoughtful look. "Perhaps. But change isn't always bad. Sometimes, it's necessary for growth." Then I frowned. "But what if I'm making things worse?" "Then we fix it," Aelira said simply.

Then on what felt like the last day of our time together, Aelira announced she had stabilized the rift.
"I can return to my era now," she said. "And I might be able to send you back to yours." Then hope surged within me. "Really? You can send me home?" Then Aelira hesitated. "I can try. But there's a risk. And the temporal disruption around you is... volatile. And if the attempt fails, you could be scattered across time again—or worse." Then I swallowed hard. "I don't have much of a choice, do I?" No," Aelira said softly. Then she began to activate the portal, with her hands moving deftly over her wrist device. Then the swirling energy grew brighter, and more intense, until it filled the entire cave with its glow. "Step into the light," Aelira instructed. "And whatever happens, remember this: You're stronger than you think. So trust yourself." Then I nodded, with my heart pounding. "Thank you, Aelira. For everything." And with that, I stepped into the portal. And the world dissolved around me in a blaze of light, and I braced myself for whatever came next.

(Moses & The Israelites)

Then moments later the world came into focus in a haze of heat and dust. And the first thing that I noticed was the overwhelming noise of voices raised in a mixture of panic and elation. Then the second thing was the sheer number of people surrounding as men, women, children, livestock— and I mean thousands of them, all moving as one. And standing at the front of it all, with his arms raised to the heavens, was a man whose presence radiated authority and faith. "Moses," Aelira murmured beside me, and her voice tinged with awe. Then I turned to look at her, and still stunned by her presence. Then when I stepped into the portal back in the Ice Age, I thought that was the end of our partnership. But somehow, Aelira had been caught in the temporal web again, tethered to my journey through time. "You're still here?" I asked, though relief and gratitude flooded my chest. Then Aelira gave me a wry smile. "Seems like time isn't finished with either of us."

Then the crowd surged forward, and Aelira and I were swept along with them and it didn't take long to figure out what was happening. And I quickly realized that Moses had led the Israelites out of Egypt, but Pharaoh's army was in hot pursuit and the Red Sea loomed ahead, an impassable barrier—or so it seemed. "What do we do?" I asked, with my heart racing as the sound of approaching chariots grew louder. "We observe," Aelira replied, with her gaze fixed on Moses. "Because this is a pivotal moment in your timeline and interfering could have catastrophic consequences." "UNDERSTOOD" I replied even though I wasn't sure but I still agreed. Then the tension in the air grew palpable, and the fear on people's faces unbearable. But as I watched Moses, his unwavering faith seemed to anchor the chaos around him. Then it happened and with his staff raised high, Moses called out in a voice that seemed to shake the very earth and then the sea began to part.

And the sight was breathtaking as the walls of water raised on both sides, creating a path through the sea. And the Israelites hesitated only a moment before surging forward, and their cries of awe mingling with the roar of the wind. Then Aelira and I followed, and the surreal experience left us both speechless as the ground beneath our feet was damp but firm, the towering walls of water shimmering like glass. "Your people," Aelira said quietly, "are capable of incredible things when driven by faith." Then I glanced at her, noting that the wonder in her usually stoic expression. "It's not just faith," I said. "It's survival. Hope. The will to keep moving, even when the odds seem impossible." Then Aelira nodded, with her gaze distant. "Perhaps that's something we can all learn from."

Then once we reached the other side, the mood shifted from terror to triumph. As the people celebrated, with their joy infectious even as exhaustion weighed heavily on them. Then Aelira and I kept to the fringes, doing our best to blend in. And I fashioned a crude robe from nearby materials, while Aelira used her advanced tech to modify her appearance slightly, making them less conspicuous. Then as the days passed, we integrated into the group, helping where we could without drawing attention. And I gathered firewood and water, while Aelira used her futuristic knowledge to treat minor injuries and ailments but despite our efforts to remain unnoticed, it wasn't long before Moses himself approached us.

"I've seen you," Moses said, his piercing eyes locking onto mine. "You and your companion—you are not of this place." Then I froze, unsure how to respond. Then Aelira, ever composed, stepped forward. "We are travelers," she said simply. "Just passing through." Then Moses studied us for a long moment, then nodded. "Many among us are strangers in a strange land. But you... you carry a weight I do not yet understand." "Sorry but we're here to help," I said quickly, desperate to redirect the conversation. Then Moses's expression softened. "Then help you shall. But be warned—this journey is not for the faint of heart."

Then over the weeks that followed, I found myself drawn to Moses's quiet strength and unshakable resolve. Despite the challenges he faced—doubt from his people, the harshness of the wilderness, the weight of his mission—he never wavered. "Moses," I asked one evening as we sat by a small fire, "how do you keep going? How do you lead when everything seems to be against you?" Then he regarded me with a thoughtful expression. "Faith, young man. Not just in the Almighty, but in the purpose that he has set before me. And when you know your path, even the darkest night cannot deter you." And then his words struck a chord deep within me because for so long, I had been lost in the chaos of time, struggling to find my way back. But perhaps my journey wasn't just about returning home. Perhaps it was about finding purpose in the places I landed.

Then Aelira, too, seemed profoundly affected by our time with Moses and the Israelites. "I've studied countless civilizations," she admitted one day as we watched the camp prepare for another day's travel. "But I've never been part of one like this. Seeing these people—how they persevere despite everything—it's... humbling."

I smiled. "Welcome to humanity." Then Aelira chuckled softly. "You're more resilient than I ever gave you credit for." Then as the weeks stretched on, I felt the familiar pull of time beginning to shift around me. Then the air grew heavy with that strange, static energy, and Aelira noticed it too. "It's happening again," she said, with her tone laced with both anticipation and dread. Then I nodded, with my heart sinking because I didn't want to leave—not yet. Because there was still so much to learn, and so much to do. But time had its own plans. And before we departed, Moses approached us one last time. "Wherever your journey takes you," he said, his voice firm but kind, "remember this: You are never truly alone. And the same force that guides me guides you as well." Then I nodded, swallowing the lump in my throat. "Thank you, Moses. For everything." Then after that, the light consumed us once more, and the world dissolved around us.

Then after the pull of time again the world reassembled around me with a strange familiarity and a dusty landscape, and a throng of people, and a leader standing at the forefront of it all. But this wasn't Moses because the man before me had a different energy—it was more youthful yet burdened, confident yet cautious.
"Joshua," Aelira whispered, appearing beside me as though she'd been there the whole time. Then her sharp eyes scanned the surroundings, instantly piecing together the context. And as we stood on the edge of an enormous encampment, the buzz of activity filled the air. And the Israelites were preparing for something big because there was a palpable tension, a mix of anticipation and determination. "This is...after Moses," I said, piecing it together myself. "Forty years in the wilderness. Joshua's leading them into the Promised Land." Then Aelira nodded, with her expression unreadable. "The end of one era, the beginning of another."

And unlike Moses, Joshua didn't have an aura of divine mysticism. And his presence was more grounded, and his leadership pragmatic. Yet, there was no denying the respect his people had for him. And wherever he walked, conversations hushed, and heads bowed. "I don't think we'll go unnoticed for long," Aelira remarked, with her gaze following Joshua as he moved through the camp and she was right because within hours, we were approached by a group of men who eyed us with suspicion. "Strangers?" one of them asked, with his hand resting on the hilt of a dagger. "We're travelers," Aelira said, with her voice calm and measured. "Passing through." Then the men exchanged glances before one of them gestured for us to follow.

And Joshua's tent was modest but well-guarded and inside, he stood poring over a map that spreaded across a rough-hewn table. Then he looked up as we entered, his piercing gaze locking onto mine. "You're not from this camp," he said simply and it wasn't a question. "No, sir," I replied, with my voice steady despite the butterflies in my stomach. "We're travelers." Then Joshua's brow furrowed. "Travelers from where?" Then Aelira stepped forward. "From far away. But we mean no harm and if anything, we'd like to help." Then Joshua studied us for a long moment before nodding. "Help, you say? Then prove it because the Lord has tasked us with taking the city of Jericho, but the path ahead is fraught with challenges and if you truly mean to aid us, you will find your place among my people."

Then over the next few days, Aelira and I integrated into the camp. And I found myself helping with the practical tasks—gathering supplies, reinforcing tents, and carrying messages. Aelira, meanwhile, used her advanced knowledge to assist with medical needs and even strategizing. And the Israelites were wary of us at first, but slowly, they began to accept us. But there was something humbling about their resilience because these were people who had endured decades of hardship, and yet their faith remained unshaken. "Do you ever envy them?" I asked Aelira one night as we sat by the fire. Aelira tilted her head thoughtfully. "Their conviction? Their sense of purpose? Yes, sometimes."

Then when the day of the siege arrived, the camp was alive with a mix of excitement and apprehension. Then Joshua gathered his people, with his voice strong and steady as he relayed the Lord's instructions: to march around the city once a day for six days, and on the seventh day, the walls would fall. And it sounded impossible like a science fiction movie, But the Israelites didn't question it. They moved as one, with their faith unwavering. Then Aelira and I joined the procession, as we blended into the crowd as best as we could. Then the first six days passed without incident, but the tension grew with each march. And by the seventh day, the air was electric.

Then as the people marched around Jericho for the seventh time, the shofar sounded—a deep, resonant call that seemed to echo through my very bones. Then the Israelites raised their voices in a thunderous shout, and before my eyes, the walls of Jericho began to crumble. And it wasn't just a collapse; it was a moment charged with divine energy, as though the heavens themselves had intervened. Then Aelira stood beside me, with her usually composed expression awash with awe. "This...this defies explanation," she murmured. "It's faith," I said, my own voice shaking. "It's power beyond anything we can understand."

Then in the aftermath, the Israelites moved into the city, with their cries of victory filling the air. And Joshua stood at the center of it all, with his face a mixture of triumph and humility. "I understand now why Moses chose him," Aelira said quietly as we watched from a distance. Then I nodded. "Because he's a leader in his own right. Different from Moses, but just as necessary." Then as we prepared to move on, I couldn't help but feel a deep respect for the people I had journeyed with. And they had shown me the strength of unity, and the power of faith, and the importance of perseverance. And then the familiar pull of time began to take hold, and the edges of the world started dissolving into light. "Where to next?" Aelira asked, with her tone both curious and resigned. "I don't know but I guess we'll find out," I replied, bracing myself for whatever lay ahead.

(Ancient Rome)

Then as the light faded, and my senses snapped into place beneath my feet, was a hard-packed dirt of a bustling street replaced by the wilderness. And the air was alive with the hum of voices, with the clatter of wheels on cobblestones, and the acrid tang of smoke from braziers. "Rome," Aelira whispered, brushing dust from her tunic-like attire because she had adapted seamlessly to every era we'd been thrown into, and her demeanor calm and observant. Then I stood there, mouth agape, marveling at the sheer scale of the city before us. And towering columns, sprawling marketplaces, and marble statues loomed in every direction, a testament to human ambition and craftsmanship. "This is...something else," I muttered. Then Aelira nodded. "Yes the heart of an empire." She replied

Then the center of activity was the Forum, an expansive plaza surrounded by grand temples and government buildings as people bustled about, with their togas and stolas swishing as they moved with purpose. And orators stood on raised platforms, and their voices ringing out with speeches that captivated passersby. Then Aelira and I weaved through the crowd, and carefully tried not to draw too much attention but despite the chaos, there was a rhythm to the city, a balance between the structured power of the Senate and the raw energy of its citizens. "It's like being inside a living machine," I said, watching a group of scribes jot down notes on wax tablets. Then Aelira smirked. "A machine fueled by ambition, conquest, and politics."

Then our attempt to blend in didn't last long because within hours, we were stopped by a group of Roman guards, and their eyes narrowing as they took in our unusual accents and mannerisms. "What brings you to the Forum?" one of them demanded, his hand resting on the hilt of his gladius. "We're travelers," Aelira said smoothly, bowing their head slightly. "Seeking knowledge of your great city." Then the guard grunted, and clearly was unimpressed. "Travelers or spies?" Then before Aelira could respond, a well-dressed man intervened. "Peace, Centurion. These two are no threat." The man introduced himself as Marcus, a senator intrigued by our apparent naivety. Whether out of genuine curiosity or an ulterior motive, he invited us to his villa for supper.

And Marcus's villa was a marvel—a sprawling estate adorned with mosaics, frescoes, and intricate fountains. As slaves moved silently through the halls, carrying trays of food and wine and despite the luxury, there was an undercurrent of tension, and a reminder of the rigid social hierarchy. "You're not from here," Marcus said as we reclined on couches in his triclinium, picking at dishes of roasted meat and honeyed figs. "Correct we are not we're from far away," Aelira replied, choosing her words carefully. "Travelers, as we said." Marcus raised an eyebrow but didn't press further. Instead, he regaled us with tales of Roman

75

politics, and the Senate's intrigues, and the empire's conquests. "There is greatness here," he said, gesturing around him. "But also fragility. Rome is an empire built on strength, yet it teeters on the edge of chaos."

Then over the next few weeks, Aelira and I became embedded in Roman life. As Marcus, was fascinated by our knowledge of the world, and he allowed us to stay in his villa in exchange for insights into foreign lands. Then I found work as a scribe, and my familiarity with Latin aiding me in transcribing scrolls. Then Aelira, ever resourceful, assisted the villa's physician, introducing rudimentary antiseptic practices that astonished him. Then we moved through the city like ghosts, observing its splendor and its flaws. As gladiatorial games in the Colosseum drew roaring crowds, with their cheers masking the brutal reality of the spectacle. And the aqueducts carried water to the city's fountains, but in the slums, disease and poverty ran rampant. "It's a city of contradictions," I said one evening as we walked along the Tiber River. Then Aelira nodded. "Greatness and cruelty often go hand in hand."

Then our peaceful existence couldn't last because one night, whispers of rebellion reached Marcus's villa. And a plot against the emperor started brewing in the shadows, and threats to engulf the city in turmoil. "You need to leave," Marcus warned us, with his usually composed demeanor cracking. "Because if you're caught up in this, you won't survive." Then Aelira and I exchanged a glance, both realizing the danger we faced. But something about Marcus's fear compelled us to stay a little longer. Then the rebellion erupted without warning, and the city descending into chaos. As fires raged through the Forum, and the air was thick with the cries of the injured and the clash of steel. Then Aelira and I moved through the chaos, helping where we could, but it was clear that Rome's veneer of control had shattered. "We need to go," Aelira urged, with her usually steady voice tinged with urgency. Then as the world around us burned, the now-familiar pull of time began to take hold. And the edges of reality blurred, and the noise of the city faded into silence. Then I looked back one last time, and the grandeur of Rome etched into my memory.

(The City of David)

Then as if the fabric of reality had been ripped apart and hastily sewn back together. I landed and when the blinding light subsided, I found myself standing on a hill overlooking a city that radiated ancient splendor. And the city was smaller than I expected, as it nestled against the rocky terrain, but its walls and structures were alive with purpose and history. "Michael," Aelira said softly, with her voice carrying a rare reverence. "This is the City of David." Then I froze. The City of David. A place I had only read about in texts and imagined through vague interpretations of history. But here it was—real, vibrant, and teeming with life.

And the city was a hive of activity and workers carried stones to fortify the walls, and artisans shaped clay into vessels, and priests performed rituals in the shadow of the Tabernacle. And every sight and sound reinforced the significance of the place because this was no ordinary city; it was the heart of a kingdom that would shape the spiritual and cultural identity of the world. "Do you feel that?" Aelira asked, her eyes scanning the bustling streets. "Feel what?" I replied, though I already knew. "The weight of this place. It's not just history—it's something more."

I nodded, unable to articulate the sense of awe that gripped me.

Then our presence, as always, drew attention because two strangers dressed in fabrics and styles unfamiliar to the time would naturally stand out. But instead of suspicion or hostility, the people seemed curious, almost welcoming. And it wasn't long before the word of the strangers reached the king himself. King David, when we met him, was not the larger-than-life figure I had imagined. He was a man—shorter than I expected, with kind but sharp eyes that seemed to see straight through me. But yet his presence was undeniable, a mix of humility and authority that commanded respect. "You are travelers," he said, his voice measured. "but from where?" Then Aelira, as always, was quick to respond. "From distant lands but we have come to learn and to aid, if we can." Then David studied us for a long moment before nodding. "Then you are welcome here. But tread carefully. The Lord watches over this city, and its purpose is divine."

Then over the next few weeks, Aelira and I became woven into the fabric of the city. And we helped craftsmen shape tools and observed the scribes as they meticulously copied sacred texts. Then the community was tightly knit, and every action imbued with a sense of purpose. And I spent hours wandering the city's streets, marveling at the ingenuity of its designs like the water channels carved into the rock, the granaries storing food for the people, and the simple yet sturdy homes all spoke of a people determined to thrive against the odds. Then one day, I found myself at the site of the Tabernacle, with its grandeur understated but no less profound. Then the priests moved with deliberate precision, with their prayers and sacrifices filling the air with a sense of solemnity.

And it was during one of these quiet moments, as I stood at the edge of the city overlooking the Kidron Valley, that Aelira approached me. "Michael," she said, with her voice unusually serious. "There's something different about this time." "What do you mean?" I asked, though I had sensed it too. "This city, its people—they're bound to a destiny far greater than themselves. But with that comes great danger. So we must tread carefully." Then I nodded, and the weight of her words settled heavily on my shoulders and I had felt it too—as the sense that this place was a pillar of history and faith, and its significance echoing through time.

Then as the days turned into weeks, I saw firsthand the challenges of ruling such a city. And David was not just a warrior but also a leader, mediating disputes, planning defenses, and nurturing his people's faith. And I watched as he prepared for battles against external threats and dealt with internal dissent, and his resolve unwavering. Then one evening, as the sun dipped below the horizon, I found myself in a quiet corner of the palace, speaking with David. "Do you believe in destiny?" he asked suddenly. "I think so," I replied, caught off guard. "Then you understand why this city must endure," he said. "Not for me, but for what it represents—a covenant, a promise." Then his words stayed with me, as a reminder of the immense responsibility he bore.

Then just as we had begun to feel a part of the city, the familiar pull of time began to assert itself. And it was always bittersweet, and leaving behind the lives and stories that we had become entangled with. Then as the light enveloped us once more, I looked back at the City of David, and its walls and people now etched into my memory. "This place," I said softly, "it's more than just a city." Then Aelira nodded, with her expression unreadable. "It's a cornerstone." And then we were gone, pulled into the unknown once again

Then the familiar tug of time tore at my core, and it dragging me and Aelira through the unseen currents of the web. Then the kaleidoscope of light and sound faded as abruptly as it had begun, and when I opened my eyes, the City of David stood before us once more. Only this time, it was different. And the air was heavy with mourning, and the streets quieter than I remembered. And the city's once-bustling heart seemed subdued, and its pulse slower, as its people lost in thought. "Michael," Aelira whispered, with her gaze fixed on the palace at the city's center. "Something's changed." And I didn't need them to tell me what. Then the weight of grief hung over the city like a shroud.

And it wasn't long before we learned the reason and that was that King David was dead the warrior poet who had united the tribes of Israel and built this city into a symbol of faith and strength was no longer. And his passing was not just a personal loss for the people—it was the end of an era. Then in the days that followed, the city buzzed with preparations for Solomon's coronation. And the young king was to step into his father's monumental legacy, and the weight of expectation was palpable. "I never thought we'd see this," I said to Aelira as we stood near the palace gates, watching the procession of dignitaries and priests. "But time doesn't play by our rules," she replied, with her expression unreadable. "So we're here for a reason, Michael. We always are."

Then Through a series of circumstances that I can only describe as fate—or perhaps divine intervention—we found ourselves granted an audience with the new king. And Solomon was younger than I expected, and his face a mix of boyish uncertainty and the budding confidence of a ruler. "You are travelers?" he asked, with his voice calm but curious. "Yes we are," Aelira said with a respectful bow. "From faraway lands. We wish to offer our service to the city in these times of transition." Then Solomon studied us for a long moment before nodding. "My father spoke of strangers who appeared in our city once before, who carried wisdom and insight beyond their years so perhaps you are like them." Then the comment sent a chill down my spine. Could David have remembered us after all? Or had tales of our presence been passed down through the palace halls?

Then over the next weeks, we became silent observers to Solomon's ascension. And the ceremony itself was a spectacle, filled with music, sacrifices, and proclamations of loyalty from the people and tribal leaders. But the true test of Solomon's reign came in the days that followed. As he began to take the reins of leadership because I saw a young man grappling with the enormity of his role. And he sought counsel from elders, listened to disputes among the people, and spent hours in prayer at the Tabernacle. Then one evening, I found myself speaking with Solomon alone, in a rare moment of candidness in the midst of his responsibilities. "What do you think makes a great king?" he asked me, with his eyes searching mine. Then I hesitated. "A great king is one who listens to his people and seeks wisdom beyond his own understanding." Then he nodded, with his expression thoughtful. "Right and my father was a man of war but I wish to be a man of peace. But peace requires a wisdom I do not yet possess." "You will find it," I said, though I wasn't entirely sure how.

Then as always, Aelira had a way of cutting through the noise. And one night, as we stood on the rooftop of a humble home overlooking the city, they turned to me with a serious expression. "Michael, Solomon is more than just a king. He's a symbol of transition—a bridge between the old ways and something entirely new." "What do you mean?" I asked. "David built the foundation, but Solomon will build the legacy. This city, this kingdom—it's not just about the present. It's about what will come after." Then I nodded, feeling the weight of their words.

Then as the days turned into weeks, I saw Solomon begin to grow into his role and he made bold decisions, some of which were met with resistance, but he remained steadfast. And his wisdom, even at this early stage, was beginning to shine through. Then one day, I witnessed him render judgment in a particularly contentious dispute between two women. And his decision, both clever and compassionate, left the people in awe. As it was clear that this young king was destined for greatness. Then just as I felt we were beginning to understand this new era, the familiar pull of time began to make itself known again. And I had grown used to it by now, but it never got easier.

As the light began to envelop us, Then I looked back at the city, and its walls and people now etched deeper into my heart. Then Solomon stood on the palace steps, with his figure framed by the setting sun, as a symbol of hope and renewal. "We'll be remembered," Aelira said softly as the pull grew stronger. "I hope so," I replied, though I wasn't sure if it was true. And then we were gone, and swept away to another time, another place, leaving the City of David—and its new king—behind.

(World War 3)

Then after we were pulled through the web again my body felt like it was being unraveling and reassembling all at once, as my mind struggling to grasp where—or when—we'd land. Then when the chaos settled, I found myself on uneven ground, surrounded by an eerie silence punctuated by distant booms. And the air was thick, and reeking of smoke and scorched metal. Then I staggered to my feet, and brushed ash from my clothes. "Aelira?" I called, with my voice weak. "I'm here." As she appeared from behind a mound of rubble, with her face pale but composed. "Where are we now?" I asked, taking in the desolate landscape as towering ruins of what might have once been skyscrapers jutted out of the ground like skeletal remains and fires burned in the distance, and the sky was a sickly orange-gray, choked with pollution. Then Aelira's expression darkened. "We're in the middle of World War Three."

And the words hit me like a punch to the gut because I'd read about wars, studied history, and seen depictions of past battles. But this... this was something else entirely. This was a war of the future. With massive, mechanical drones that flew overhead, with their shapes sleek and ominous. And soldiers in advanced armor moved like shadows, with their weapons firing and bursts of energy that melted through steel. "For me, this is the future," I said, trying to steady my breathing. "But for you...?" Aelira's gaze was distant, her voice tinged with a sorrow "It's history to me. And this war happened centuries before my time. And I learned about it in school, and read about it in books. But seeing it again... it's worse than I imagined." Then I blinked at her, struggling to process what she was saying. "Wait. You're saying this war—World War Three—wasn't just a chapter in history for you? But you've been here before?" And she nodded, with her face shadowed with memories. "I grew up in the aftermath of this war."

Then the days blurred as we moved through the ruins, and dodging patrols and scavenging what we could find. And the war wasn't confined to armies and battlefields; because it engulfed everything and everyone and civilians cowered in makeshift shelters, with their faces hollow with despair. Then one day, we stumbled upon a group of refugees hiding in an underground subway station. And their leader, was an older woman named Margot, who greeted us with cautious suspicion. "Are you here to fight?" she asked, with her voice hoarse. "No," Aelira said firmly. "We're just passing through." Then Margot's gaze softened, and she gestured for us to join them. Then that night, we listened to their stories—and we heard about their homes being destroyed, families torn apart, and a desperate struggle to survive in a world turned hostile.

Then as we sat by the flickering firelight, Aelira shared snippets of her perspective. "This war wasn't just about nations fighting nations," she explained.

"It was about resources, survival. And the Earth had been pushed to its limits—climate collapse, overpopulation, dwindling resources. So humanity fought over what was left." Then I shivered, because the enormity of it all sinked in. "Did it end?" I asked. "I mean, did anything good come out of it?" Then Aelira hesitated. "It ended," she said carefully. "But not before humanity nearly destroyed itself. And the rebuilding was slow, painful. And even centuries later, the consequences of this war still lingered in my time."

Then as time passed we couldn't avoid the conflict forever and one day, while scavenging for food in the ruins of a grocery store, a firefight broke out. And it was a group of soldiers that clashed with a resistance faction, with their weapons lighting up the darkened sky. "Stay low!" Aelira hissed, pulling me behind a fallen beam. Then I crouched beside her, and my heart pounded as energy blasts zipped overhead. Then the soldiers moved with terrifying precision, and their advanced armor making them nearly unstoppable. But the resistance fighters were resourceful, using the environment to their advantage. Then we watched in tense silence until the chaos subsided. And when it was over, the ground was littered with bodies—both soldiers and civilians caught in the crossfire. And "That's the reality of this war," Aelira said quietly. "There are no winners. Only survivors."

Then the longer we stayed, the more I understood the hopelessness that hung over this world. And people clung to scraps of food, shelter, and humanity, with their lives reduced to a constant fight for survival. Then one night, as we sat on a rooftop overlooking the shattered city, I turned to Aelira. "Why does this war matter so much to you and why do you know so much about it?" Then she stared at the horizon, with her eyes reflecting the distant fires. "Because it shaped everything that came after," she said. "It was the turning point humanity had to choose between annihilation or evolution. And the scars of this war forced us to change, but it came at a terrible cost."

Then as the weeks passed, I couldn't help but wonder what this meant for my time and if this war was in my future, or was it inevitable and could it be prevented? Then Aelira seemed to sense my thoughts. "The future isn't set in stone," she said one night as we sheltered in an abandoned building. "But every choice humanity makes leads to consequences. And your time, Michael, is closer to this war than you realize but what you do matters because it doesn't have to happen." And then her words haunted me and the weight of responsibility pressed heavily on my shoulders.

Then the world around us was unrecognizable, and even months after our initial arrival. And the skies remained perpetually clouded with ash and smoke, and the air carried the metallic tang of devastation. And the city we wandered through had become a skeletal remains of its former self, with skyscrapers reduced to jagged stumps, and streets choked with debris. But yet, amidst the chaos, life clung stubbornly to existence. And for weeks now, Aelira and I had shifted from mere observers to active participants doing whatever we could to help those struggling to survive and it wasn't about grand gestures or monumental changes; it was about small, crucial acts—like finding food, and delivering medical aid, while offering protection in this shattered world, but those acts could mean the difference between life and death.

Then our days began to revolve around a network of survivors who had banded together in an abandoned subway system beneath the city. And the tunnels, once a hub of human connection, had become a lifeline for those seeking refuge from the relentless conflict above. Then Margot, the leader we had met in our first weeks here, had taken us into her group despite her initial wariness. And her keen intelligence and unyielding resolve had earned her the respect of the other survivors. "This isn't just a war between nations," Margot explained one evening, her voice heavy with exhaustion. "It's a war against humanity itself. And we're caught in the crossfire." Then her words stayed with me as we worked to fortify the tunnels, transforming them into a hidden sanctuary. Then Aelira and I used whatever knowledge we could muster to improve the group's chances.

Then one of the most critical tasks was finding food and clean water because supplies were scarce, and scavenging missions were perilous. And the streets above were patrolled by soldiers and drones, on both sides treating any civilian as a potential threat. Then on one particularly harrowing mission, we ventured into the ruins of a supermarket and the shelves were almost entirely stripped bare, but Aelira's sharp eyes spotted a stash of canned goods hidden beneath fallen debris. "Stay alert," she murmured as we worked to free the cans. And The warning proved prescient. Then moments later, the whirring of a drone's engines echoed through the aisles. As we froze, barely daring to breathe as the machine's red eye scanned the area. "Move slowly," I whispered, as my heart pounded hard. Then we managed to slip out through a side entrance, and the drone none the wiser. But the close call left us shaken. "Every trip is a gamble," I said once we were back in the tunnels. "And every success is a victory," Aelira countered, with her determination unshaken.

Then despite the grim circumstances, moments of humanity shone through the darkness. As a young boy named tommy, no older than ten, had taken to following Aelira around, with his curiosity outweighing his fear. "Where are you from?" he asked one day, and his wide eyes fixed on her. "Far away," Aelira replied with a faint smile. "Further than here?" "Much further." And tommy's innocent questions reminded me of what was at stake. And this wasn't just about survival; it was about preserving the flicker of hope that still burned in people like him. Then one night, I found myself telling stories to a small group of children huddled around a dim lantern. And I spoke of my own time, of places untouched by war, and of dreams worth chasing. Then their faces lit up, and but only for a moment, and I realized how much power there was in something as simple as a story.

Then Aelira and I often talked during the quiet moments, exchanging insights about the worlds we came from. "This war is a pivotal point," she futher told me one evening. "and its effects ripple through time in ways that are hard to quantify or explain but it's why my world looks the way it does." Then I studied her face, illuminated by the faint glow of a makeshift lantern. "Does knowing how it ends make it easier or harder for you?" "Both," she admitted. "Because the knowledge is a burden, but it's also a guide. And if I can help even a few people here, it feels worth it." And her words resonated with me deeply despite being trapped in this timeline, and the uncertainty, but I found a strange sense of purpose.

Then the weeks turned into months, and the group of survivors grew stronger under Margot's leadership. But the war continued to escalate, and the battles above grew more closer and more violent. Then one day, while helping to transport an injured woman to a safer part of the tunnels, we were caught in a bombardment. And the ground shook violently, and debris rained down around us. "Go, go, go!" Aelira shouted, with her voice cutting through the chaos. And we barely made it to safety, as the tunnel collapsed behind us and the woman survived, but the close call left us all shaken. "This can't go on forever," I said to Aelira later, with my voice heavy with exhaustion.

"It won't," she replied. "But how it ends is still being written." Then as the days dragged on, I began to feel the familiar sensation of the temporal pull building again. And it was faint at first, like a whisper at the edge of my awareness, but it grew stronger with each passing day. "Aelira," I said one night as we sat on the cold concrete floor of the subway station, "I think it's happening again." Then she nodded, with her expression unreadable. "It's time," she said simply. "But do you think we'll ever stop moving through time?" "I don't know," she admitted. "But wherever we go next, we'll face it together." Then as the pull intensified, I looked around at the faces of the survivors that we had come to know and care for and leaving them felt like abandoning a part of myself, but I knew we couldn't stay. And Then the world began to blur, and the sounds of the subway station faded into nothingness.

(1st Grade Again)

After I stopped being pulled in the void the world snapped back into focus, but not the world I'd expected. But instead of chaos or ancient ruins, I was staring down at a pair of small, chubby hands clutching a crayon. Then my breath caught because my hands weren't just smaller—they were *mine*, but decades younger. So, I looked around, with my heart racing fast. And rows of tiny desks stretched out before me, and they were filled with children no older than six or seven and bright posters covered the walls, proclaiming things like *"Learning is Fun!"* and *"Be Kind!"* in cheerful fonts and the smell of crayons, glue, and construction paper was thick in the air but how because this was impossible. Then it wasn't until I saw the chalkboard that the full weight of what was happening hit me. And the date scrawled in loopy handwriting read, *September 15, 2015.*

"Michael? Are you paying attention?" Then the voice froze me in my seat. And I turned slowly toward it, with my mouth dry. And standing at the front of the class, holding a book in her hands, was Aelira, but she wasn't the time-traveling companion I'd come to know. She was wearing a floral dress, with her hair tied back in a neat bun, and looking every bit the part of a first-grade teacher. Then her eyes met mine, and for a moment, they widened with recognition.

"Michael, would you like to answer the question?" she asked, with her tone even but with an edge of curiosity. Then the rest of the class turned to look at me, and their giggles and whispers filling the room. Then I swallowed hard, feeling my cheeks flush. "Uh... sorry, I didn't hear the question," I mumbled, my voice higher and squeakier than I remembered. "That's all right," she said with a small smile. "Let's try to focus, okay?" Then As she turned back to the chalkboard, I slumped in my seat, with my mind racing because this had to be a dream, or some cruel trick of time because how could I be here, in *this* moment of my life? And why was Aelira here, too?

And the next few days were a surreal blend of familiarity and confusion. As my childhood friends surrounded me, with their faces unchanged by time, and I was back in my family's modest home, where everything seemed smaller than I remembered. And my parents didn't seem to notice anything strange, and they treated me as though I was still their six-year-old boy. But Aelira—she *knew*. Because during storytime one afternoon, I caught her glancing at me, with her expression thoughtful. And after the other students had left for recess, she called me to her desk. "Michael," she began, with her voice soft but firm, "do you feel... different?" Then my breath caught. "What do you mean?" I asked cautiously. Then her eyes searched mine, and then she leaned in slightly, lowering her voice. "I think we've met before." Then I froze, unsure of how to respond. "What do you mean?" She hesitated, then said, "I don't know how to explain it, but there's something about you that feels... out of place. Like you don't belong here. Am I wrong?" then I shook my head slowly, and the weight of her words settling on me. "No," I whispered. "You're not wrong."

Then as time moved on I realized that living as my first-grade self was both a blessing and a curse. And on one hand, the pressures of adulthood were gone, and replaced by the simple concerns of recess games and spelling tests then on the other hand, my adult mind struggled to adjust to the limitations of my tiny body and the expectations of a six-year-old. "Michael, you need to color inside the lines," Aelira reminded me one day during art class, with her tone teasing. And I couldn't help but laugh. "I've done this before, you know." Then she raised an eyebrow. "Oh, really? Care to elaborate?" then I hesitated, realizing how absurd my situation sounded. "Let's just say I've had practice," I replied vaguely. Then her lips twitched into a smile, but she didn't press further.

Then as the weeks passed, I noticed subtle ways how Aelira tried to connect with me because she would drop hints during lessons, like asking questions that seemed aimed more at my adult mind than my classmates'. "Michael," she asked during a history lesson, "what do you think it was like to live during ancient Rome?" Then I blinked, caught off guard. "Uh... probably difficult," I said carefully. "Lots of political drama." Then her eyes sparkled with amusement. "An interesting perspective," she said, moving on. And I couldn't shake the feeling that she was testing me, trying to confirm what she already suspected.

Then one afternoon, as the other students were busy building block towers, Aelira pulled me aside. "Michael," she began, her tone serious, "I need to know the truth. Who are you?" Then I hesitated, debating whether to tell her everything. But the look in her eyes—the same look I'd seen countless times in our travels—convinced me.
"You already know," I said quietly. Then her eyes widened, and for a moment, she looked as though she might deny it. But then she nodded slowly. "You're... not supposed to be here, are you?" "Neither are you," I pointed out.

Then she let out a soft laugh, as the tension eased slightly. "Fair enough. But why here? Why now?"
"I don't know," I admitted. "It's like the timeline is pulling us to these moments for a reason." Then from that moment on, we shared a silent understanding. And in the classroom, she was still my teacher, guiding me through the daily routines of first grade. But in the quiet moments, we spoke as equals, trying to piece together the mystery of our predicament. Then one evening, as I sat at my tiny desk finishing a math worksheet, she leaned down and whispered, "We'll figure this

out, Michael. We always do." And her words gave me a sense of hope I hadn't felt in weeks.

Then just as I was beginning to adjust to this strange new life, the familiar sensation of the temporal pull began to stir. And I felt it first as a faint tug in the back of my mind, then as a growing certainty that our time here was coming to an end. Then one afternoon, as the class was practicing their handwriting, Aelira caught my eye. And she gave me a small nod, and I knew she felt it too. "It's time," she said softly as the world around us began to blur. Then the room faded away, and the cheerful chatter of children got replaced by the hum of the unknown. Then once again, we were pulled into the currents of time, and our journey was far from over.

Then when I landed, the scene was hauntingly familiar: a room filled with pint-sized desks, vibrant posters shouting cheerful encouragements like *"Believe in Yourself!"*, and the faint smell of crayons and construction paper. And I stared down at my hands—small, pudgy, and unmistakably childlike. Then my heart sank. "No," I muttered, with my voice high-pitched and squeaky. "Not again why am I here again." "Michael, are you with us?" Then I froze at the sound of Aelira's voice again. Then slowly, I turned to see her standing at the front of the room, looking like every bit of the first-grade teacher she had been the last time I'd found myself in this bizarre scenario. With her floral dress, perfectly tied bun, and warm smile would have fooled anyone else into thinking she was just another ordinary educator. But not me. I knew better. Then her eyes met mine, and for a brief moment, I saw it—the spark of recognition, fleeting but undeniable.

Then as time passed the days felt like a cruel replay of my previous ordeal. The same math problems, the same recess games, and the same awkward struggle to fit in with six-year-olds while harboring the mind of a grown man. But this time, it was different. And Aelira wasn't just pretending to be oblivious. She was watching me carefully, as though waiting for me to make the first move. Then during storytime one afternoon, she read aloud from a children's book about a lost boy trying to find his way home. And the other kids listened, while giggling at the silly illustrations, and her gaze flicked to me. "Sometimes," she said softly, her voice carrying a weight the children wouldn't understand, "we have to go back to where it all began to understand where we're meant to go." Then I stared at her, as the words sank in like stones because she knew something.

Then it wasn't until a week later that we had our first real conversation as the other kids were at recess, leaving the classroom empty except for the two of us because I lingered behind, pretending to struggle with tying my shoe. "Michael," she said finally, breaking the silence. "You know why you're here, don't you?" Then I looked up at her, startled. "If I did, I wouldn't still be here," I said, with frustration creeping into my voice. Then she nodded slowly, while pulling a chair beside me and sitting down. And for a moment, she seemed to hesitate, then said, "I think the answer lies in *you*. Something from this time—this version of yourself—is holding you here." Then I frowned, trying to make sense of her words. "But why would I need to come back to *this*? What could possibly be so important about first grade?" Then her eyes softened. "Sometimes the simplest moments shape us in ways we don't realize. Perhaps there's something you left unfinished. Something you need to remember." She said

Then over the next few days, Aelira began subtly guiding me to look deeper into my surroundings. And she encouraged me to interact more with my classmates, and to pay attention to the little details of my day. And at first, it felt pointless because how could playing with blocks or sharing snacks possibly hold the key to my predicament? Then one day, during art class, I stumbled upon something that stopped me cold. As we were instructed to draw a picture of our families. And as I picked up a crayon and began sketching, a memory surfaced—vivid and sharp. Then my six-year-old self had drawn this same picture before: a crude house with stick-figure versions of my parents, my sister, and me. But this time, I noticed something strange. And in the corner of the drawing, my younger self had added a small, smiling figure but I didn't recognize—a woman with long hair and a kind face. "What's that?" Aelira asked, leaning over my shoulder. Then I hesitated, and then pointed at the figure. "I don't know. But... I think I've seen her before." And then her expression grew thoughtful. "Perhaps you have," she said cryptically.

Then the more I thought about the drawing, the more memories began to surface—small, fleeting moments that I had long forgotten. Then I remembered sitting in this very classroom, feeling lonely and uncertain, and how my first-grade teacher had always seemed to know exactly what to say and how to make me feel better. "She was *you*," I said one day, as the realization hit me like a freight train. "You were my Ist grade teacher back then, weren't you?" Then Aelira's smile turned to a bittersweet smile. "Right and I've been connected to you for longer than you realize, Michael. But it's not just about me because there's something *you* need to realize about yourself."

Then with Aelira's guidance, I began to see what I had been blind to before. And my time in first grade wasn't just about reliving the past because it was about confronting the fear and self-doubt that had taken root in me at a young age. Then one day, during recess, a group of kids was playing tag, and I hesitated to join in because of the fear of rejection, and of being too slow or clumsy, loomed large. "Go," Aelira urged, with her voice gentle but firm. "You can't move forward until you stop holding yourself back." Then as I took a deep breath, I joined the game. And at first, it was awkward and uncomfortable, but soon, I found myself laughing, running, and forgetting my fears.

Then on my last day in the classroom, Aelira pulled me aside. "You've grown more than you realize, Michael. And this isn't just about time travel. It's about healing." Then I frowned, still unsure. "But why now? Why did I have to go through all of this to figure it out?" Then she smiled. "Because sometimes, the only way forward is to revisit the places that shaped us and you were meant to find strength in your past, so you could face whatever comes next." Then as the day ended, I felt the familiar tug of the temporal pull, and it was stronger than ever. Then I looked at Aelira, and she nodded knowingly. "Goodbye, Michael," she said softly. "And until we meet again." Then the world blurred around me, and as I was swept away into the unknown, I carried with me a newfound sense of purpose—and a lingering gratitude for the woman who had guided me through the maze of time.

(Parallel Universes)

Then I came to, a feeling of relief as my limbs felt longer, stronger, and heavier, like they belonged to me again. So I glanced down and flexed my fingers—and there was no tiny, pudgy digits this time because my adult body had returned. But relief was fleeting. And Aelira stood nearby, with her arms crossed and a inscrutable expression on her face and we were in a setting I didn't recognize but it was a bustling urban street bathed in a neon glow of 2025 but yet something felt... off. "Welcome back, Michael," she said with a cryptic smile. "Or rather, welcome *forward*."

I was too disoriented to parse her words fully. "Where are we now?" "Your time," she replied, while gesturing to the world around us. "But not your world."

Then the truth hit me slowly because we weren't in *my* 2025 and then I realized that Aelira had led me through a version of my city that was hauntingly familiar but yet disturbingly altered. And billboards advertised products that I'd never heard of, and stores I used frequently were replaced with strange new businesses, and the faces of people walking by were both recognizable and alien. "This is an alternate reality," Aelira explained as we passed a newsstand where the headlines blared about a political leader that I'd never voted for. "A version of your world shaped by decisions you didn't make." Then I stopped short. "Why are we here? What am I supposed to learn from this?" then her smile turned enigmatic. "You'll see."

And the first alternate version of my life hit me like a punch to the gut as we arrived at a sprawling suburban neighborhood where the houses looked plucked straight out of a real estate commercial. And a family I recognized but didn't know intimately lived in one of them and then I noticed that it was me—or at least, a version of me but this Michael was polished, confident, and successful. Then he stepped out of the house in a tailored suit, and kissed a woman I didn't recognize on the cheek, and waved goodbye to two bright-eyed kids before driving off in a sleek car. "Who is that?" I asked, even though the answer was obvious. "That's you," Aelira replied. "In a reality where you pursued a different career path." Then I stared, feeling equal parts of envy and unease because this life looked idyllic on the surface, but as we followed this version of me through his day, cracks began to show because the work consumed him and his relationships were strained. And by the time we left, I wasn't sure whether I envied him or pitied him.

Then the next reality was far less comfortable because this time, I found myself in a dimly lit apartment, cluttered with unwashed dishes and piles of laundry and the alternate version of me here was disheveled, bitter, and defeated because he spent his days scrolling aimlessly through the internet and his nights drinking away his frustrations. "What happened to him?" I asked, my voice hushed. Then Aelira's expression softened. "In this world, you let fear dictate your choices and you avoided risks and stayed in your comfort zone... until it became a trap." Then I felt sick watching this version of me spiral out of control and it was a cautionary tale, and one that hit far too close to home.

And perhaps the most jarring reality was the one where I didn't exist at all when Aelira led me through a city where my presence—or absence—had rippled through the lives of others. Friends I cherished lived entirely different lives. Projects I'd worked on never came to fruition. And even my family seemed changed, their faces etched with a sadness I couldn't quite place. "Every life touches others in ways you can't always see," Aelira said quietly as I struggled to process the scene. And the more realities we visited, the more I began to question Aelira's motives because her knowledge was too precise, and her guidance too pointed and she seemed to know more about me than I was comfortable with, and her answers to my questions were always just vague enough to keep me guessing. "Why are you doing this?" I demanded one evening as we sat on a park bench in yet another alternate version of my life. "To help you," she replied simply. "But why *me*? Why not someone else?" Then she hesitated for a fraction of a second and just long enough for me to catch it. "Because you're important, Michael and more than you realize." But I didn't buy it. "You're not just a time traveler, are you?" Then her eyes flicked to mine, and for a moment, I thought I saw something ancient and unfathomable lurking beneath her calm exterior. "That's not the right question," she said finally. "Then what is?" I said then her smile went faint, and almost sad. "Why are *you* the one being pulled through time?" she finally said and that question haunted me as we continued to traverse alternate realities. And each version of my life seemed designed to teach me something—to show me my strengths, my flaws, and the impact of my choices. But the answers felt just out of reach, like a puzzle missing its final piece.

But through it all, Aelira remained a constant, while guiding me with a mixture of patience and cryptic wisdom. Yet the more time I spent with her, the more convinced I became that she wasn't telling me everything.
Who—or what—was she? And why did I feel like the answer to that question would change everything? Then when the pull of time deposited me again, it wasn't in 2025 or any familiar year I'd seen before. This time, the skyline of a city I recognized shimmered with futuristic skyscrapers and holographic displays and now it was 2030—five years ahead of where my life had been uprooted from. But this wasn't my future. Or at least, not a single, consistent version of it. And Aelira was there, as always, with her expression a mix of bemusement and something deeper I couldn't yet name. "Ready for the next lesson?" she asked. Then I

frowned. "Lesson? That's what this is?" Then she smiled faintly, and for the umpteenth time, I felt the nagging sense that she was holding something back.

And the first version of 2030 she took me to was dazzling because the me of this world—let's call him Future-Michael—was everything I'd dreamed of becoming. He stood at the head of a sprawling tech empire, overseeing projects that reshaped industries as crowds of reporters clamored for his insights, and his name was spoken with reverence and as future Michael walked through the glass-walled of his headquarters "my" company, I couldn't help but feel a pang of envy because this Michael exuded confidence, and his every move purposeful and assured. But yet as we shadowed him, cracks began to appear in the façade and Future-Michael was alone, and disconnected from the world outside his corporate bubble. And relationships were transactional, and conversations were hollow. Then when he stared out of his penthouse window at night, his eyes betrayed a deep loneliness. Then Aelira turned to me as I watched him in silence. "Would you trade everything you have now for this?" And the question lingered in the air as we moved on.

Then the next 2030 was a dystopian nightmare as the streets were shadowed by towering walls, and the air buzzed with the sound of drones patrolling the skies and this version of the future felt more like a prison than a society. And I found myself working as a teacher in this world, but not the kind of educator that I'd ever imagined. My role here was to indoctrinate, and to enforce loyalty to an oppressive regime and the classroom was sterile, with the children's faces void of curiosity. "Why are you showing me this?" I asked Aelira, with my voice sharp with anger. "Because this is what happens when fear dominates," she replied calmly. "When innovation and progress are stifled in favor of control." And I hated the version of myself who could have existed here—a man complicit in the oppression of others and it was a sobering reminder of the moral choices that shape our lives.

Then the next jump took us to a 2030 so idyllic it felt like stepping into a dream with clean energy powered vibrant cities, and people moved with purpose and joy, and a sense of unity radiated from every interaction. And this time, I wasn't the central figure. I was a minor player in a world that didn't need me to succeed. And my contributions had been meaningful, but the world's progress didn't hinge on my existence. "Not every path revolves around you," Aelira said gently as I observed a bustling market filled with laughter and trade. "But sometimes, the greatest impact is letting others thrive." And it was a humbling realization, and one that left me with a mix of peace and uncertainty.

Then the more alternate futures we visited, the more questions I had about Aelira and about her knowledge of these timelines because they were too precise, and her guidance was too intentional. And I knew that she wasn't just a traveler, swept along like me but she was orchestrating something. "You know too much," I said finally, as we stood on the edge of a gleaming, sky-high garden in another version of 2030. "You're not just here by chance."

Her lips quirked into that maddening, cryptic smile. "I've told you before, Michael. I'm here to help you."

"Why me?" I pressed. "What makes me so special?" Then her gaze turned serious, like the weight of centuries—or perhaps millennia's—flickering in her eyes. "Because your choices matter more than you realize. And because I see the threads of time more clearly than you do." And it wasn't an answer, not really, but it was the most direct she'd ever been so far.

Then in one final alternate 2030, Aelira brought me to a version of my life where I wasn't Michael at all—at least, not in the way I recognized because my name, my face, and even my memories were different. And I was a leader of a grassroots movement, fighting to preserve the freedoms and rights of a crumbling society. And this me was bold, inspiring, and selfless, but yet he carried a burden so immense it threatened to crush him and by watching him, I felt a strange mix of pride and sorrow. "This version of you is remarkable," Aelira said, her voice almost wistful. "But he's also alone. Leadership often demands sacrifice." Then I turned to her, frustrated. "What are you trying to show me, Aelira? That no matter what I choose, I'm destined to suffer?" Then she shook her head. "I'm showing you that every choice has consequences. And that you're more resilient than you think."

Then as we left the final 2030 behind, my suspicions about Aelira reached a boiling point because she wasn't just guiding me; she was shaping me, molding me into something—or someone—for reasons I couldn't yet understand. "You're not telling me everything," I said as we stood in the swirling void between timelines. "No," she admitted, her tone almost gentle. "But you're not ready for the whole truth yet." Then the admission left me reeling because what was I being prepared for? And who—or what—was Aelira, really? And those answers felt maddeningly close, but yet just out of reach. Then my journey continued, and when time released its grip on me once more, I found myself standing in 2035 and the air was sharp, carrying an energy that felt both familiar and foreign. And Aelira was there, steady as always, and her enigmatic demeanor was a frustrating constant. "This is 2035," she said. "Your future—or at least, fragments of it." And I had long since given up questioning how she managed to navigate these leaps with such precision because her knowledge surpassed even the most improbable guesses.

Then as I observed the first reality that she had led me into it was bleak and the sky was thick with ash, and the ground trembled under the weight of destruction as smoke rose from the rubble of collapsed buildings, and distant sirens wailed like ghosts, and it didn't take me long to realize where I was. This was World War 3, a horrifying glimpse of what could come to pass. Then I saw different versions of myself scattered across this hellscape—one huddled in a bunker, another leading a ragged band of survivors scavenging for food. And each version of me looked more haunted than the last, and their eyes carrying the weight of choices that led to this devastation.

"Is this real?" I asked Aelira, with my voice barely above a whisper. "It's real in the sense that it could be," she said, with her tone measured but grave. "and if certain paths are taken, this is what might unfold." And the enormity of her words sank in as we moved through the desolation. And families clung to one another in makeshift shelters, as soldiers trudged through the debris with weary determination, and the air was thick with despair. "Why show me this?" I demanded. "Why force me to witness this?" "Because your choices matter, Michael," she replied, her voice sharper now. "More than you understand. The decisions you make ripple through time in ways you can't yet comprehend."

Then after the devastation, the next 2035 was a startling contrast because the world here was vibrant and alive, and a harmonious blend of nature and technology. And cities shimmered with a sustainable energy, and people moved with purpose and joy. And in this version, I was a teacher—not of history, but of philosophy and my classroom was filled with students eager to learn, and their eyes bright with hope. Then Aelira stood silently at the back, observing me as I taught. "This is a world built on the right choices," she said later, as we strolled through a lush urban garden. "Collaboration, empathy, and foresight created this reality." Then I couldn't help but feel a pang of pride at the role I had apparently played here, but her words haunted me because the implication was clear: and if I could help build a world like this, I could just as easily destroy it.

Then another reality showed me in a world caught in a different kind of turmoil because in this 2035, I was a corporate titan, wealthy beyond imagination but morally bankrupt and the world around me was starkly divided—opulence for the few and suffering for the many. And this time, Aelira didn't need to explain the lesson because watching the chaos unfold—the riots, the desperation, and the systemic inequality—was enough to drive the point home because my indifference in this timeline had cost countless lives, and the guilt of it pressed heavily on my chest.

Then we returned to the timeline of World War 3, but this time, Aelira revealed something new and she brought me to a battlefield where soldiers clashed in brutal combat, and their faces grim with resolve. And amid the chaos, she gestured to a younger version of myself—just a face in the crowd, yet pivotal in ways I didn't yet understand. "Do you see him?" she asked, her voice low. "That's you. And your choice in this moment will determine whether this war begins or ends." Then I stared at the younger me, and my heart pounding hard. He—or I—

was locked in a fierce debate with a commanding officer and it was clear that the decision being made here had far-reaching consequences. "What choice?" I asked, my voice trembling. Then Aelira turned to me, with her gaze piercing. "Whether to escalate or de-escalate. Whether to lead with courage or with fear because it always came down to that." And the weight of her words settled over me like a shroud because my choices had consequences beyond anything I'd imagined. Then as we moved through these alternate lives, I couldn't shake the growing suspicion that Aelira wasn't just a guide because she was too invested, too precise in her timing and her lessons.

"Why do you care so much?" I demanded one evening again, as we sat overlooking a shimmering cityscape in yet another version of 2035. "Why are you so determined to show me these things?"

Then her expression softened, and for a moment, she looked almost sad. "Because I've seen what happens when people like you fail to realize their importance because the threads of time are fragile, Michael. And you... you're one of the weavers." And her answer left me with more questions than answers, but one thing was clear: Aelira wasn't just another traveler or guide like I suspected but she was something more—something I wasn't sure I could fully trust. And in the end, she brought me to a crossroads—a literal one, in yet another alternate version of 2035. And there were two paths before me, and each leading to a different future. "This isn't just symbolic," she said. "This is real. The decisions you make from here on will shape the course of history." Then I stared at the paths, with my mind racing with everything I'd seen because the weight of responsibility was almost too much to bear. "I don't know if I'm ready for this," I admitted. "No one ever is," she replied. "But that doesn't make it any less necessary." She replied.

(The Time Keepers)

Then as I reached my next destination the air was still with no sound, no scent, and no sensation met me as I opened my eyes and it felt as though I were suspended in a void. But slowly, the blankness gave way to a shimmering landscape—and a city bathed in a light that wasn't sunlight but seemed to emanate from everywhere and nowhere at once. "This," Aelira then said as she appeared beside me, with her voice steady, "is the Omniverse. The city outside of time." Then I blinked, trying to make sense of my surroundings because the architecture was unlike anything I had ever seen with towering spires intertwined with crystalline structures that glowed faintly, as though alive. And the streets were paved with shifting patterns, morphing beneath our feet as if charting the steps of history itself. And the People—or beings—moved gracefully through the city, and some were human-like, while others ethereal, with their forms shimmering as though they were made of starlight.

"Welcome to the seat of the Time Keepers," Aelira continued, gesturing to the expanse before us. "This is where the threads of existence converge and where the fabric of reality is woven." Then my mind spun with questions, but I found myself speechless because the city pulsed with an energy that felt both alien and deeply familiar. Then as we walked, I noticed intricate murals adorning the walls of the towering buildings, and each depicting moments from history—some I recognized, and others I couldn't place. "Every thread, every moment, and every choice," Aelira explained as we passed one particularly striking mural of a war I didn't recognize, "is observed, preserved, and sometimes... corrected." "Corrected?" I echoed, with my voice cracking slightly. Then Aelira glanced at me, with her usual enigmatic expression softening. "Not all paths are meant to be taken, Michael. And not all who walk them understand the weight of their steps."

Then our path led us to a grand hall at the center of the city and it was circular, with its domed ceiling reflecting an endless starfield. And around the room sat beings of immense presence, with their forms indistinct yet commanding and they radiated authority, as their mere existence was a testament to their power. "These are the Time Keepers," Aelira said, with her tone reverent. "They oversee the flow of existence, while ensuring balance across all realities." Then I felt impossibly small under their collective gaze. As their voices echoed in my mind—not in words, but in impressions, emotions, and concepts too vast for language. And then, to my shock, Aelira stepped forward and addressed them with confidence. "Greetings, Council," she said, with her voice clear. "I bring Michael, the Weaver of Threads, as foretold." Then I stared at her, stunned. Weaver of Threads? Foretold? What was she talking about?

Then the room dimmed as Aelira turned to face me and for the first time, I saw her not as a guide or a companion, but as something far greater as she stood taller, with her form shimmering with an otherworldly light. "You've suspected, haven't you?" she said, with her voice layered with tones that resonated deep within me. "I'm not just a traveler. I am the Head of the Time Keepers." Then her words hit me like a tidal wave. Aelira, the enigmatic woman who had guided me through countless moments in history, was far more than I had imagined. "Why?" I managed to choke out. "Why all of this? Why me?" Then Aelira's gaze softened. "Because you are more important than you realize, Michael because you're not just a man caught in the web of time—you are a pivotal figure in your era, and someone whose choices shape not only your reality but countless of others."

Then she gestured, and the air shimmered, forming a tapestry of light and motion and it depicted my life—and moments I recognized and others I didn't and I saw myself as a boy, then as a soldier, then as an old man giving a speech to a vast crowd. "In your time," Aelira explained, "you are a catalyst. Your actions inspire revolutions, unite divided nations, and alter the course of history in ways no one else can." Then I shook my head, overwhelmed. "But I'm just... me. I'm no one special." Then Aelira stepped closer, with her expression unwavering. "That's what you've always believed. But the truth is, every step you've taken, every decision you've made, has prepared you for this and the threads of time have been converging around you, Michael. You are not ordinary."

Then I thought back to the trials I had endured—the battles, the losses, the victories, and the heartbreak. And each moment had felt random, like I was being tossed around by an indifferent universe. "Everything you've shown me," I said slowly, "wasn't just history lessons, was it? They were tests." "Yes," Aelira admitted. "You needed to see the consequences of certain choices. To understand the fragility of existence and the weight of your role in preserving it." Then the realization hit me like a hammer because the horrors of war, the beauty of peace, and the devastation of indifference—all of it had been preparing me for something greater.

Then the Time Keepers surrounded me, with their presence both comforting and intimidating. And Aelira stepped aside, allowing their collective voice to resonate within me. "Michael," they intoned, "you stand at the crossroads of history. And the choices you make will ripple through time, shaping the destinies of countless lives. So will you accept your role as the Weaver of Threads?" Then I hesitated, because the enormity of the responsibility weighed heavily on me. But then I thought of everything I'd seen, every life I'd touched. And I couldn't turn away now. "I'll do it," I said, with my voice steady. "I'll try." Then as the vision of the city began to fade, Aelira placed a hand on my shoulder.

"This isn't the end, Michael. It's only the beginning. Trust yourself, and remember: even the smallest thread can hold the weight of a universe."

Then the Omniverse shimmered with its eternal glow, and a unearthly brilliance that neither waxed nor waned. And the city outside of time thrummed with an energy that defied comprehension, as a constant reminder that this place operated beyond the limitations of human existence. Then I sat with Aelira on the edge of a reflecting pool that mirrored not only our faces but the constellations of countless realities above. And her demeanor had shifted since revealing her role as the head of the Time Keepers and the enigmatic confidence I had grown accustomed to was still there, but now it was tempered by a solemnity that I had never seen before. "Michael," she began, with her voice a melody of authority and gentleness, "you've seen the tapestry of time, the intricate web that connects all things. But there is one thread that weaves through it all, a force that transcends even the Omniverse itself: the Creator of the Universe." Then I blinked, taken back. Because in all our travels, and in all the impossible things I'd witnessed, Aelira had never spoken of divinity so explicitly.

Then I leaned forward, with curiosity overcoming my hesitation. "You mean God? The God of the Bible?"

Then Aelira smiled faintly, with her gaze fixed on the pool. "Yes but not like you think, because though many names are given, and many understandings are formed but the Creator of the Universe, and the Architect of Time—it is this being who set the foundations of existence and entrusted me with the role I now carry." Then her words hung in the air, as heavy as the silence that followed. And I struggled to wrap my mind around that idea. "You were chosen?" I asked finally. "Chosen by... Him?" "Yes," she said, her tone reverent. "Long before I became what I am now, I was like you—a traveler through the threads of time. But my journeys were not random; they were a test of faith just like yours, with endurance, and purpose. And at the end of my path, I was brought here to the Omniverse and I was entrusted with the sacred duty of preserving the balance of time."

Then I studied her, trying to reconcile the woman that I had traveled with—and the one who had fought beside me, comforted me, and challenged me—with this exalted figure she now revealed herself to be. "But why?" I asked. "Why you? Why would the Creator need someone to manage time? Isn't that... His domain?" "It is," she said, nodding. "But the Creator works through His creations and time is both a gift and a trial, and a framework within which free will can flourish. And my role is not to control time but to guide and protect it, and to ensure that free will does not unravel the fabric of existence." Then she turned to me, with her eyes piercing but yet compassionate. "The Creator entrusted me with this role because I understood the weight of time, and the beauty and fragility of choices. And now, Michael, you are being called to understand it too."

Then I frowned, while still grappling with the enormity of her revelation. "But why involve me? I'm just... a human. How can I possibly fit into all of this?" Then Aelira's expression softened. "I was just a human too and you underestimate yourself to much, as many do. But the Creator does not choose the proud or the perfect; He chooses those willing to learn, to grow, to act in faith. And your journey has been no accident, Michael because every moment, and every struggle, has been preparing you for this." Then she gestured to the Omniverse around us, the ever-shifting brilliance that seemed to pulse in time with her words. "You were brought here not only to witness but to participate, to see the impact of your choices across the tapestry of existence. And now, you stand at a crossroads, as I once did." Then I couldn't help but ask, "What happened to you? How did you... become this?" Then Aelira smiled wistfully, with her gaze returning to the reflecting pool. "Because when my journey ended, I was brought before the Creator in a place beyond description. And I was shown the threads of time, and also the lives I had touched, with the moments that I had influenced without even realizing it. And then I was asked: Would I accept the responsibility to protect what I had come to understand?" Then her voice wavered slightly, and the memory clearly a profound one. "It was not an easy decision". To accept meant giving up the life I had known, to become something more and less than human. But it also meant serving a purpose greater than myself and I chose to say yes." Then she looked at me, as her eyes shimmered with an intensity that seemed to pierce my very soul. "Now you face a similar choice, Michael to become what I am but in your own way, and to embrace your role as a shaper of time and history." Then I felt a lump rise in my throat. "But what if I fail? What if I make the wrong choices?" Then Aelira placed a hand on my shoulder, with her touch warm and grounding. "The Creator does not expect perfection, Michael. He only asks for faithfulness and you've already seen what happens when choices go astray and you've seen the devastation of war, the beauty of redemption, and the cost of apathy So now you are prepared, even if you don't realize it." And then her words were a balm to my fears, but they also carried a weight that I couldn't ignore. "So... this is why you've been with me," I said slowly. "Not just to guide me through history but to prepare me for this moment." "Yes," she said simply.

Then we sat in silence for a while, and the enormity of her revelation settling over me like a heavy cloak. Then finally, I found my voice. "If the Creator trusts you," I said, "then I trust you too." Then Aelira smiled, a rare warmth in her expression. "Thank you, Michael. But remember, your journey is not about me or even the Time Keepers. It's about the lives you will touch, the choices you will make, and the legacy you will leave behind." Then she stood, offering me her hand. "Come. There is more for you to see." And as I took her hand, the Omniverse seemed to pulse with approval, as though the city itself acknowledged the path that I was beginning to understand.

(Peace on Earth)

Then the portal before us shimmered with an iridescent glow, and its swirling depths unlike any I had seen before. Then Aelira and I stood side by side, with her expression calm yet reverent, as though this moment was the culmination of everything she had prepared me for. "Are you ready, Michael?" she asked, with her voice a gentle echo in the space around us. Then I took a deep breath. "As ready as I'll ever be. Where does this one lead?" Then Her smile turned enigmatic, as a glimmer of something both knowing and hopeful in her eyes flickered. "To the end. Or rather, to a new beginning." Then without another word, we stepped through.

And the sensation of crossing through this portal was different from all the others—it was way more softer, and almost soothing, as though I were being cradled by the very fabric of existence. Then when we emerged, the world around us took my breath away. And we stood on a hill overlooking a sprawling city that seemed to radiate light, and not just from its buildings but from the very air itself. And towers of shimmering crystal reached skyward, with their forms elegant and organic, as though grown rather than built. And parks and rivers wove through the city like veins of life, and the people—and I mean a countless amount of people— moved with an air of harmony and purpose that I had never seen before in my life. "Is this Earth?" I asked, barely able to believe what I was seeing.
"Yes," Aelira said. "Earth, as it will be when humanity has finally achieved peace."

Then as we descended into the city, the details of this transformed world became clearer. And the streets were alive with laughter and conversation, but there was no sense of chaos or disorder. And people of all backgrounds and appearances mingled freely, with their faces open and unguarded. And technology was everywhere, yet it blended seamlessly with nature as floating vehicles glided silently above streets and lined with trees bearing fruits of colors I couldn't even name. and buildings shimmered as though they were alive, while adapting their shapes and colors to the environment and the needs of the people within. "How?" I asked, my voice tinged with awe. "How did they do it? How did we do it?" Then Aelira gestured to a group of children playing nearby, as their laughter rang out like music. "It began with them—with education, compassion, and a willingness to break the cycles of fear and greed. Then humanity learned to prioritize the well-being of the all over the desires of a the few. And it wasn't easy, Michael believe me because it took centuries of struggle, and countless of mistakes, and unimaginable losses. But in the end, they chose love."

Then we spent weeks exploring this world, and time in this place seemed to flow differently. And the concept of hours and days felt almost irrelevant in a society that had transcended the need for urgency. Then I spoke with scientists who had unlocked the secrets of sustainable energy, while ensuring that no resource was ever depleted. Then I met artists who used their work to heal hearts and inspire minds, and their creations celebrated not for profit but for the joy they brought. And I listened to leaders who governed not only with power but with humility, and their decisions guided by the collective wisdom of the people. And everywhere I went, I saw the same thing: unity.

"It's like... a dream," I said to Aelira one evening as we watched the sun set over the city, and its rays refracting through the crystalline structures to paint the sky in hues of gold and violet. "It was a dream," she replied. "And for millennia's, it was only a dream. But dreams have power, Michael. They shape reality, just as your choices shape the future."

Then one day, Aelira led me to a grand hall at the heart of the city and inside, a council of elders awaited us, and their presence commanding yet serene. As each of them seemed to embody the wisdom of ages, with their eyes filled with a depth that made me feel both seen and understood. "Welcome, Michael," one of them then said, with their voice resonating like a melody. "You have traveled far to witness this moment, and you have been allowed." Then I nodded, unsure of how to respond. "And now we are what humanity can become," the elder continued, "when fear is replaced by understanding, when division is replaced by unity. And you are here to carry this vision back with you, to remind your time that peace is not an impossible ideal but a choice—a choice that must be made every day." Then as we left the hall, their words echoed in my mind because for so long, I had been focused on surviving the chaos of my journey, and trying to understand why I had been chosen for this strange odyssey. But now, I began to see the bigger picture. "and it's not just about me, is it?" I said to Aelira. "All of this—the time travel, the lessons—it's about humanity as a whole."

Then she nodded, with her expression soft. "Yes and you are a part of the whole, Michael because your choices ripple outward more than mines ever did, and influencing those around you, just as theirs influence you. And every act of kindness, every moment of courage, and every decision to choose love over fear— it all adds up. That is the lesson the Time Keepers wanted you to learn." Then as our time in this peaceful future drew to a close, I felt a strange mix of emotions: hope for what humanity could achieve and a deep sense of responsibility for the role I might play in getting there. "It's time," Aelira said one morning, her tone gentle but firm. "Time for what?"

"To return," she said. "To your life, your choices, your world. You've seen what's possible, Michael. Now it's up to you to help make it a reality." Then we stood before a portal, with its light warm and inviting. And as I turned to face her, I saw something in her eyes—a quiet pride, as though she knew I was ready. "Thank you," I said, my voice thick with emotion. "For everything." Then Aelira smiled. "Thank you, Michael. For choosing to see." And then, I stepped through the void of time, carrying the vision of peace in my heart and the knowledge that every choice mattered more than I had ever realized.

(Back Home)

Then the transition through the final portal felt softer, and almost tender, like the universe itself was welcoming me back to my own time. Then the swirling light that had become so familiar faded slowly, while leaving behind the walls of my living room. Then I blinked, disoriented. And the silence was almost deafening compared to the vibrant symphonies of peace that I had just witnessed. And my eyes drifted to the clock on the wall. **12:30 PM.**

It took a moment for the weight of that to settle in. I had been gone for what felt like years—and decades, even—wandering through the folds of time, and witnessing epochs of history and glimpses of the future. But yet, here, in the present, only four hours had passed since I first touched the mysterious artifact that started it all. And I stood in stunned silence, and the faint hum of my refrigerator was the only sound anchoring me to reality.

Then at first, everything seemed exactly as I had left it because the light filtered through the blinds at the same angle. And the half-empty coffee cup still sat on the table while my phone buzzed with a mundane notifications, and that tethering me to the ordinary. But I was not the same. The Michael who had left this room was naïve, driven by routine and a narrow view of life's possibilities. Now, I carried the weight of countless lives, choices, and lessons in my mind and heart and my hands trembled slightly as I picked up the coffee cup, and its lukewarm contents was a stark contrast to the warmth of the future that I had seen.

Then I didn't drink it but instead, I poured it down the sink and stared out the window, and my reflection superimposed over the familiar view of my street as cars passed by, neighbors mowed their lawns, and kids played. And it was all so... normal. And yet, I couldn't help but wonder: was the seed of a better world already planted here?

Then the days that followed were a strange blend of routine and transformation. And on the surface, I returned to my regular life—work, errands, catching up with friends. But beneath that veneer in my mouth, every decision I made was infused with a deeper awareness. And when I passed a homeless man on the street, I didn't just walk by but instead, I stopped, and offered him a meal, and I listened to his story. And the act felt small compared to the grand visions of unity that I had seen, but Aelira's voice echoed in my mind: **Every choice ripples outwardly.**

Then at work, I found myself stepping into a more collaborative role. And I listened more intently, encouraged my team, and sought to uplift others rather than push my own agenda. Then to my surprise, these small shifts created an atmosphere of trust and productivity that I hadn't thought possible. And in my personal relationships, I mended old rifts as I reached out to family members and I hadn't spoken to them in years, but humbled by the knowledge that this time is fleeting conversations that once seemed difficult now felt necessary and healing. But not every day was easy. And the challenges of the modern world hadn't magically disappeared. Because there were still arguments, misunderstandings, and moments of doubt. But now, I approached these obstacles with a better sense of purpose. And I remembered the countless civilizations that I had witnessed—and their triumphs and failures—and I understood that progress was rarely linear. And even the most harmonious societies had struggled and stumbled before finding their footing. And the key, I realized, was resilience as the determination to keep moving forward, and to keep choosing love, compassion, and understanding and even when it seemed impossible.

Then after 10 years had passed in real time the world outside my window was different now, and though not in the way I once feared. And since I returned from my journey through time. Ten years of choices, both small and large, made with intention and purpose. And now, as I stand here in the warmth of an afternoon sun that feels brighter than it ever did before, and I see a world transformed—not perfect, but undeniably better. And the hum of distant laughter drifts in through the open window, while mingling with the faint scent of blooming flowers from the community garden below as children played in the park across the street, with their carefree giggles as a melody that would have been drowned out by the roar of sirens and gunfire in the future I once glimpsed and World War 3 did not happen.

And in the years since, I've seen so much progress. Like renewable energy becoming the norm, and reducing the environmental strain that once loomed as a crisis as education reform has created opportunities for countless children, giving them the tools to build a better tomorrow. But it's not just the big changes that stand out to me. It's the small moments—the acts of kindness and connection that I see every day. And a few months ago, I watched a teenager help an elderly neighbor carry groceries up the steps. And the sight brought tears to my eyes, not because it was extraordinary, but because it was so beautifully ordinary. And this is the world we've built—not perfect, but striving.

And as for me, I've found a new kind of purpose. And I still work in my community, but my focus has shifted. And I mentor young leaders now, by sharing stories of resilience and the importance of choice. And I don't tell them the full truth about my journey in fact I never told anyone—because I doubt they'd believe it—but I think they sense the depth of my conviction. And my relationships have deepened as well. As I reconnected with people I once drifted away from, and those bonds have become anchors in my life. And I've even found love—something I never thought I'd prioritize before my journey. And sometimes, I catch myself wondering what's next because the future is no longer a shadowy threat hanging over me, but a bright expanse of possibility. And I know challenges will come—we are, after all, only human—but I also know we have the capacity to overcome them. And Aelira showed me the vast tapestry of time, and while my thread is just one among countless of others, it's woven into something greater than I could have ever imagined. Then as the sun begun to set, casting the sky in hues of orange and pink, I feel a deep sense of peace because the world isn't perfect, but it's moving in the right direction. And maybe that's all any of us can hope for—to leave the world just a little better than we found it and one choice at a time.

www.ingramcontent.com/pod-product-compliance
Lightning Source LLC
Chambersburg PA
CBHW030346030726
47499CB00003B/920